S0-AAF-713

SLIPPERY BUSINESS

Gunn watched the soap bubbles form as the last bucket of hot water was poured into the enormous bathtub. He paid the bellboy who had carried the water up for him, locked the door, and undressed. Then, just as he stepped into the water, the door swung open. There stood Caitlin O'Toole.

"What are you doing here?" Gunn asked.

At first Caitlin was unable to speak. "I . . . I just came in for a bath," she said weakly.

"But the door was locked."

Caitlin held up a key. "I gave the bellboy two dollars for it." Then, with a mischievous smile, she closed the door behind her and began to undress. "But I *did* come in for a bath. And as you can see, that bathtub is clearly big enough for both of us."

BOLT

An Adult Western Series by Cort Martin

#10: BAWDY HOUSE SHOWDOWN   (1176, $2.25)

#11: THE LAST BORDELLO   (1224, $2.25)

#12: THE HANGTOWN HARLOTS   (1274, $2.25)

#13: MONTANA MISTRESS   (1316, $2.25)

#14: VIRGINIA CITY VIRGIN   (1360, $2.25)

#15: BORDELLO BACKSHOOTER   (1411, $2.25)

#16: HARDCASE HUSSY   (1513, $2.25)

#17: LONE-STAR STUD   (1632, $2.25)

#18: QUEEN OF HEARTS   (1726, $2.25)

#19: PALOMINO STUD   (1815, $2.25)

#20: SIX-GUNS AND SILK   (1866, $2.25)

Available wherever paperbacks are sold, or order direct from the Publisher. Send cover price plus 50¢ per copy for mailing and handling to Zebra Books, Dept. 1914, 475 Park Avenue South, New York, N.Y. 10016. Residents of New York, New Jersey and Pennsylvania must include sales tax. DO NOT SEND CASH.

BY JORY SHERMAN

GOLD SHAFT

GUNN

#26

ZEBRA BOOKS
KENSINGTON PUBLISHING CORP.

ZEBRA BOOKS

are published by

Kensington Publishing Corp.
475 Park Avenue South
New York, NY 10016

Copyright © 1986 Jory Sherman

All rights reserved. No part of this book may be repro-
duced in any form or by any means without the prior
written consent of the Publisher, excepting brief quotes
used in reviews.

First printing: October 1986

Printed in the United States of America

This one's for Robert Vaughan, with thanks.

Chapter One

The town was no more than a cluster of buildings clinging to the side of the timber-strewn hill, certainly not one which had been laid out in any sort of master plan. Instead, it looked almost as if some of the wood had slid down the side of the hill to form, purely by chance, a collection of roughly hewn, false-front buildings; a saloon here, a bootmaker there, a hotel, a smithy, a livery stable. Most of the structures in town were built from the logs which were readily available on the hillside, and it was from that windfall that the town took its name: Deadwood.

It was getting on to evening on a day in early November, and snow was falling in the higher elevations, though Deadwood was experiencing only a cold, drenching rain. The roads were turning into quagmires, and the horses which passed by pulled their hooves from the cold, sticky mud with little sucking sounds. Even the boards by which the pedestrians crossed the streets were covered with a slippery patina of sodden mud.

No one ventured outside unless they had to. It was just too cold and wet and miserable. That's why it seemed so unusual that a woman would be outside, standing quietly behind the corner of the Deadwood Saloon, studying the street with intense brown eyes. She wore a man's hat, and a coat with the collar upturned, but if anyone passed by closely enough they could easily see that it was a woman, young, pretty, and dark-haired.

Across the street from where she was standing, a man came out of the livery stable, hurried across the road, then stood on the front porch of the saloon. Here he was somewhat sheltered from the cold rain by the saloon's overhang.

The saloon was warm and dry inside, and from the warm, dry interior, a heavyset, bald man came to stand just on the other side of the batwing doors. The solid doors hadn't been put up yet, and probably wouldn't be until early December. That was because the saloon owner believed that having solid doors deterred business. The man who was inside the saloon was wearing a white apron, and he wiped his hands with a towel.

"Coach comin' in, Harry?" he asked of the one who was standing on the porch.

"Yeah," Harry answered. He blew his nose, then stuck his handkerchief back in his pocket. "Peterson came over from the post office a while ago, said he seen it up on the highest cut-back. I reckon it'll be here in a minute or two."

"You think he'll be on it?"

"I don't know, Alves, I guess we'll just have to wait and see," Harry replied. He sniffed. "We're not going to have to wait too long though, there he is."

The coach appeared at the east end of town, turned

off the cut-back which led down from the mountain, then onto Deadwood's main road. The coach was at the far end of the street, about a quarter of a mile away, but the driver's snapping whip and piercing whistle could be heard quite clearly by those in front of the saloon. The team of horses, aware now that their long, arduous journey was nearly over, pulled hard in the harness as the driver guided them around the wagons and log-loaded mule-sleds which clogged up the road. A moment later the driver pulled back on the reins and set the brake, stopping the stage in front of the saloon.

By the time he stopped, more than a dozen people had congregated in front of the saloon to watch the arrival, and they stood there in silence staring at the snow-dusted, mud-spattered, green and yellow coach. The horses who had pulled the stage stood breathing heavily, their rubbery nostrils sending out great clouds of vapor to float away in the cold air. There were two other horses tied on back of the stage; a spotted pony and a Tennessee Walker.

"Hello, Peterson, we got mail," the driver said, throwing the pouch down to the postal clerk.

"Any passengers?"

"One," the driver said. The driver climbed down from his seat and poured snow from the crown and brim of his hat, residue from his time in the higher elevations. He looked toward the interior of the coach.

"Deadwood, mister," he said. "This is the end of the line."

The stage door opened, and a tall, well built man stepped off the stage, his gunmetal-gray eyes narrowed, his shirt bloody.

"Much obliged, mister," the driver muttered in an awestruck tone.

Gunn wondered why everyone was eyeing him so closely. There was some reward-paper out on him, yes, but he was reasonably certain it hadn't reached here. Anyway, these weren't the curious stares of someone who had seen a picture on wanted posters . . . this was something entirely different. And one of those staring most intently, he noticed, was a young woman. She was standing apart from the others, obviously not associated with them, but her eyes were as fixed on him as theirs were.

Gunn walked around to the back of the stage and untied the Tennessee Walker. The horse's name was Esquire.

"You be puttin' your horse in the livery?" Harry asked.

"Yes."

"I'm the liveryman. Name's Harry Weiner. I'll come across with you and get your horse took care of, then I'll come see to the team."

"Obliged," Gunn said. Gunn led Esquire across the street, following Weiner into the stable. The stable was dry, and relatively warm, due to the collective body temperature of the several horses that were being boarded. Gunn unsaddled Esquire, then rubbed his forehead. "What kind of feed you got?" he asked.

"Hay, and grain, some oats and corn," Weiner answered.

"Oats and corn, and do a good job currying him," Gunn ordered.

"Yes, sir. Be extry."

The tall man nodded, said nothing.

Gunn looked back toward the stage he had just come in on. Despite the rain, most of the people who had come to greet his arrival were still there, and still staring across the street at him. "What's the matter with this place?" Gunn asked. "Don't you get any strangers here?"

"Not many. But that ain't why everybody's gawkin' at you, mister."

"Why, then? My fly open?"

"Gal in town raisin' a ruckus. Sent for the U.S. Marshal. We was wonderin' if you was him."

"No. But he's not coming. That's his horse tied to the back of the stage. Maybe you should put it up and someone will come for him, pay you board."

"You killed the marshal?" Weiner asked. He felt a moment of uneasiness, and he stepped back into the shadows to stand next to a pitchfork.

"No, but he died in my arms," Gunn said. Without any further explanation he tossed a pair of cartwheels to the bewildered liveryman, then walked back toward the saloon.

As Gunn crossed the street and approached the saloon, those who were gathered on the front porch suddenly found reason to leave. Some went into the saloon, others moved on down the board sidewalk. The woman who had been watching him merely slipped back into the shadows, her dark eyes flaring with unspoken questions as Gunn stepped up onto the porch.

11

Gunn pushed through the batwings and stepped inside. The clank of glasses, the hoarse, throaty conversations, the whiffle of cards . . . all stopped abruptly as he took a table near the stove, at the side, with his back to the wall. He stretched his legs toward the Franklin, and the heat from the stove began to knock away the chill. He unbuttoned his sheepskin coat and let it fall open, placed his hat on the edge of the table, and waited for the bartender.

The heavyset man who had spoken with Harry Weiner earlier was now behind the bar, polishing glasses. He looked toward Gunn, and realizing that he was going to have to go to him, put down the towel and glass. Reluctantly he left the bar and walked to the table. He was nervous and fidgety as he approached.

"Ye . . ." he stumbled and coughed, then started again. "Yes, sir? Can I get something for you?"

"A bottle of your best whiskey . . . a bill of fare if you've got it," Gunn said. Gunn's words echoed back to him. The only sound in the entire place was the roar of the fire in the stove, and by contrast, it was nearly deafening.

"We got whiskey. Cookie can burn you some beef. We got beans, wormy potatoes, turnips, rutabagas, beets."

"Have him bring me a thick steak, beans."

"Mister, I hope you eat quick and get gone. We don't want no trouble here."

"Well, I'm as peaceable as the next feller," Gunn said. "Drier than most."

Alves walked to the kitchen door to deliver Gunn's order, then went behind the bar. Gunn looked around

12

at the others in the saloon, but as his gaze caught theirs, they would look away. A little pocket of gas, trapped in one of the logs being burned in the stove, exploded with a loud snap, and everyone in the saloon jumped. Gunn chuckled quietly. Whatever it was that had this town spooked, it had really done its job.

Alves came back to the table and put a bottle of whiskey before Gunn. Gunn picked it up and examined the label. The label was white, the printing was red and blue.

"Canadian Prime," Gunn said, reading the label. "I've never heard of this brand."

"That's what we pour here. Take it or leave it."

Gunn poured a shot, then held his glass toward the barkeep. He tossed the whiskey down in one swallow.

For a second, Gunn couldn't breathe. He even had the fleeting thought that he may have been poisoned. The whiskey was like fire, like taking a swallow of coal oil then setting it ablaze with a lucifer. Gunn's eyes began to water, and his face flushed pink as salmon. He was aware that the other patrons in the saloon were watching him closely. Finally, his breath came back to him, and he sucked in air through an enflamed throat.

"You better pay me now," Alves said. "Five bucks for the grub, four more if you keep the bottle. So far you owe me a buck."

By now Gunn realized that the whiskey wasn't poison . . . it was just incredibly bad. He pulled six dollars from his pocket and gave it to Alves, sliding the bottle back with the money.

"Bring the grub and a pail of beer," he ordered.

"Beer's green."

"Well, what's everybody else drinking in here?"

"We got some dandelion wine."

"Bring that."

"Five bucks a bottle."

"Here's your five bucks," Gunn said. "But if it's no bettern' your whiskey, I'm taking it back." Gunn slid the whiskey bottle across the table also, as if anxious to get every trace of the liquor away from him.

Sullenly, Alves took the bottle and empty glass back to the bar with him. A man at the bar whispered something to Alves, then stood up and looked toward Gunn. He was a heavy-set, burly man, wearing a peaked, battered gray Stetson. He had a low-slung pistol strapped to his leg. He hitched up his pants and crossed the room to stand at Gunn's table. From this distance Gunn could see that he had porcine blue eyes, and three days of beard stubble over a pocked chin.

"You don't like the whiskey they serve here, mister?"

"Not much."

"Well, maybe you ain't so damn much either."

"That your opinion, Jack?"

"My name ain't Jack, and yeah, that's my opinion."

"Fine," Gunn replied, the single syllable dripping sarcasm.

"Looks to me like you got some explainin' to do. What happened to Newman?"

"Who?"

"Mike Newman, the U.S. Marshal from Rapid City."

14

"Was that his name?" Gunn noticed that everyone in the saloon was watching him, listening to him. In the window he saw the woman who had watched him arrive on the stage.

"Damned right it was his name. Stage driver said you might of killed him. Don't you even bother to find out the name of people before you kill them?"

"I didn't kill him. But somebody did. Fact is, he whispered the name of the man who shot him before he died."

The hardcase who was bracing Gunn stepped back a pace, as if someone had rapped him across the mouth with a slab of raw meat.

"You got that name, stranger?"

"I got it," Gunn said. "Right here." He tapped a finger on his temple several times, and winked.

"Look here, mister, don't get smart with me."

The hardcase's hand started drifting toward the butt of his pistol.

"You want to tell me your name, mister?" Gunn asked flatly.

The man's hand stopped about halfway toward the butt of his gun. "My name? What difference does that make?"

"Like I said, I like to know the name of the men I kill," Gunn said coldly.

At that moment, the woman outside rushed into the saloon. She was dripping wet but oblivious to her own condition. She was hysterical, and she pointed at the man who was bracing Gunn.

"His name is Hank Meadows!" she screeched. "He was one of the men who got my pa drunk and dragged him out of here, never to be seen again.

15

Shoot him, mister! Shoot him dead!"

Meadows grabbed the woman, then slapped her hard. "Crazy bitch!" he shouted.

Gunn leaped to his feet, took three long strides, then rocketed a fist square into Meadows's chin. His neck snapped back as his head recoiled from the blow, and he dropped like a sack of meal. The woman moved around behind Gunn, her face blooming red with marks of the slap.

Meadows got up smiling, and Gunn was somewhat taken aback. He had hit Meadows hard enough to stun a bull, and yet Meadows was on his feet.

"Mister," Meadows said with a soft chuckle. "I'm gonna clean your plow good, then I'm gonna settle accounts with the woman."

"Mister, you oughtn't to've done that," Alves said. "Ain't no one in these parts ever seen Meadows get whipped."

"They're about to see it now," Gunn said, and he snapped a quick, slashing left into Meadows's face. It was a good, well hit blow, but Meadows just flinched once, and laughed a low, evil laugh.

"Fight! They's a fight in the saloon!" someone shouted across the batwing doors, and within a few seconds there were twice as many people in the saloon as there had been when Gunn threw the first punch. Though Gunn was concentrating on Meadows right now, in the back of his mind he wondered where all the people had come from. It wasn't as if they were out on the street, and yet here they were, gathered in a large circle to watch Hank Meadows and the stranger go at it.

"Five dollars says Meadows drops the stranger,"

someone said.

"I don't know, I've seen fellas who look like this stranger. You ask me, he's tough as rawhide. I'm goin' with the stranger."

"You gone crazy? Meadows ain't never been whipped."

Meadows rushed Gunn then, and Gunn stepped aside, avoiding him like a matador sidestepping a charging bull. And like a charging bull, Meadows slammed into a table, smashing it to kindling. He turned and faced Gunn a second time. A hush fell over the men in the saloon now, as they watched the two men in the ring formed by the crowd. They were watching the fight with a great deal of interest. They knew it would be a test of quickness and ability against brute strength, and they wanted to see if the stranger could handle Meadows. Gunn and Meadows circled around for a moment, holding their fists doubled in front of them, each trying to test the mettle of the other.

Meadows swung, a clublike swing which Gunn leaned away from. Gunn counterpunched, and again he scored well, but again, Meadows laughed it off. As the fight went on, it developed that Gunn could hit Meadows at will, and though Meadows laughed off his early blows, it was soon obvious that there was a cumulative effect to Gunn's punches. Both of Meadows's eyes began to puff up, and there was a nasty cut on his lip. Then Gunn caught Meadows in the nose with a long left, and when he felt the nose go under his hand, he knew that he had broken it. The bridge of his nose exploded like a smashed tomato and started bleeding profusely. The blood ran across

Meadows's teeth and chin.

Gunn looked for another chance at the nose, but Meadows started protecting it. Gunn was unable to get it again, though the fact that Meadows was favoring it told Gunn that the nose was hurting him. So far Meadows hadn't connected. The big man was throwing great swinging blows toward Gunn, barely missing him on a couple of occasions. As yet, Gunn was untouched.

After four or five such swinging blows, Gunn noticed that Meadows was leaving a slight opening for a good right punch, if he could just slip it in across his shoulder. He timed it, and on Meadows's next swing, Gunn threw a solid right, straight at the place where he thought Meadows's nose would be. He hit it perfectly and had the satisfaction of hearing a bellow of pain from Meadows for the first time.

Meadows was obviously growing more tired now, and he began charging more and swinging less. Gunn got set for one of his charges, then, as Meadows rushed by with his head down, Gunn stepped to one side. Like a matador thrusting his sword into the bull in a killing lunge, Gunn sent a powerful right jab to Meadows's jaw. Meadows went down and out.

"Get him out of here," Gunn said, and a couple of men grabbed hold of Meadows's unconscious form and dragged him away.

The cook came out of the back with Gunn's food. He dropped it unceremoniously on the table.

"Mister, you better hightail it out of here," he said. "Meadows has friends. When he comes to, he's liable to bring company back to help him wipe the floor with your carcass."

18

"He's right," the woman said. "This place isn't safe."

Gunn sat down to the table and looked at his food.

"Please, come with me," the woman invited. "I must talk to you."

"Not yet. I want to eat my supper," Gunn answered. "Barkeep, where's that wine I paid for?"

"Who is that fella?" someone at another table asked.

"I don't know, but if I was Meadows, I believe I'd be careful 'bout comin' back here, even if I had an army with me. Look how cool he is just sittin' there, eatin' his supper."

"Did you ever think you'd see ole Meadows handled like that feller handled him?"

"Hell, look at him. He didn't even get his hair mussed up."

Gunn walked over to the bar and got a second glass, and a jar of peppers. He returned to his table and poured a glass of wine for the woman, then opened the jar of peppers and pulled one out. He cut the pepper up onto his beans.

"I saw you watching me when I got off the stage," Gunn said.

"Yes," she said.

Gunn cut a piece of steak and slipped it into his mouth. "Pardon me for eating like this, but I haven't had anything since noon yesterday. You'd be the one who sent for the marshal?"

"Yes," she said. "My name's Nancy. Nancy Venable. I need help, mister. I was counting on the marshal to help me, but it's too late for that. You're my only chance now."

"I'm not a lawman," Gunn said. "Fact is, I try and stay away from the law as much as I can. What you ought to do is send to Rapid City for another marshal, only tell him what happened to the first. Maybe he'll be more careful gettin' here."

"Please?" Nancy begged. "Would you at least listen to my story?"

"All right," Gunn said, moved by the girl's sense of desperation. "I guess I can do that."

He hadn't heard a woman's voice in over a month. Nancy Venable's sounded like music to his ears.

Chapter Two

"It's about my father, Louis Venable," Nancy began. "Last month some men got him drunk, then took him."

"Took him? What do you mean? Took him where?"

"I don't know where, that's just it. They took him away somewhere, and he hasn't been seen since. And except for Hank Meadows, the man you just beat up, I haven't seen any of the other men, either. But I would recognize them if I ever saw them again. Believe you me, I would recognize them."

"Is that why you sent for the marshal?"

"Yes," Nancy said. "I wanted him to investigate, to find out where my father is. I don't even know if . . . if he is alive or dead," Nancy said. Tears came to her eyes, and Gunn handed her his handkerchief. Nancy sniffed, and wiped her eyes.

"What did your father do?" Gunn asked.

"Do? He didn't do anything. They had no right to . . ."

"No, I didn't mean that," Gunn interrupted. "I

21

mean what was his profession? What type of work did he do?"

"Oh, he was a miner," Nancy said. "And my father wasn't the first miner to disappear, either. There have been others. As soon as anyone shows the first sign of . . ." Nancy suddenly stopped talking and looked around the saloon. She realized then that everyone was listening to her. "I've said enough," she said. "Unless you'd be willing to help me. Would you? I can pay you. I can pay you well."

"I don't want your money," Gunn answered. "But maybe your pa went of his own accord."

"No!" Nancy said resolutely. "Never! He hated those men, what they were doing."

"And what, exactly, were they doing?"

Every man in the saloon fixed Nancy with a menacing stare, and Nancy cringed under their glare. "I've said too much in this place," she said. She saw that Gunn was now washing down the last of his food with the wine. "You've finished eating, please, come with me and I'll tell you more."

Gunn stood up, and the scrape of his chair across the floor was loud in the room. "All right," he said. "I never could resist an interesting tale, especially if it was told by a pretty girl." He looked around at the others in the saloon. "And I have seen more friendly company," he added.

It was dark by the time they went outside. The temperature had dropped by a few degrees, but there was no snow because the rain had stopped. Gunn buttoned his sheepskin coat about him, though he left the butt of his gun clear. He would have liked to turn the fur collar up, but it would have made it

22

harder to hear, so he let his neck and ears stay exposed to the cold. Nancy turned her collar up and stuck her hands deep in her pockets . . . also a luxury Gunn denied himself.

"My cabin is just beyond the edge of town here," she said. "We can walk it in about five minutes."

Gunn stepped off the plank walk, and moved to the middle of the street. The ground had hardened with the cold, so that he wasn't actually walking through mud.

"Why are you going out there?" she asked. "The sidewalk is a lot easier to walk on."

"And a lot easier to get killed on," Gunn answered.

"Are you expecting someone to ambush you?"

"Meadows might have an idea in that direction," Gunn said. "I don't figure him for the type to take a beating all that easy. And if there was anyone in the saloon listening to your story who has it in mind that he wouldn't want me to help you, then I don't want to make it easy on him to waylay me."

"Oh," Nancy said. "I guess you're right. I never thought of that." She left the walk as well, and strolled alongside him in the middle of the street.

Gunn saw some movement, a shadow within a shadow, in the space between two of the buildings. The hackles on his neck rose, and he moved his hand closer to his gun. He didn't know who or what had made the movement, but he was going to be ready just in case. The threat never materialized. Gunn knew that this could be because there was never a danger in the first place. It could also mean that whoever was hiding there was convinced that he didn't have enough of an advantage to try anything.

23

Nancy's cabin stood separated from the next, nearest house by about two hundred yards. It was small, a living room, kitchen combination, and a bedroom downstairs, with a sleeping loft above. Gunn had the opportunity to look around when Nancy lit the kerosene lantern.

"When Pa was here, I slept in the loft," Nancy explained. "Now I sleep down here." She walked over to the little stove and opened it. "The fire's gone completely out," she said.

Gunn threw some kindling into the stove, got it started, then added a few larger chunks of wood until soon there was a nice, roaring fire, and a circle of heat began to radiate from the stove. After a few minutes it was warm as toast inside, and the smell of coffee was already permeating the room. Gunn and Nancy both took off their coats and got comfortable.

"Before I tell you my story," Nancy said. "I think I ought to know your name."

"It's Gunn."

"Gunn? That's all?"

"That's enough to get my attention," Gunn said.

"Then that's name enough for me," Nancy replied. She brushed her hair back from her forehead and began her story. "There are a group of so-called businessmen in town," she said. "Hank Meadows is one of them, but there are many of them. They are whiskey drummers."

"Whiskey drummers?" Gunn said. He chuckled. "Seems to me like that's just the business that ought to come to these parts. That poison I tried to drink tonight isn't fit for man or beast."

"Canadian Prime," Nancy said. "That's the whis-

ey they peddle, and they don't let any other kind in.
ve heard that they once burned a wagonload of
ood whiskey, just to keep the market for their stuff.
nd they sell it to the Indians. Of course everybody
nows the Indians are unable to get any other kind of
whiskey, so they'll take anything."

"That doesn't seem to me like it's all that smart an
lea in this part of the country," Gunn said. "Any
ind of whiskey stirs an Indian up, but this rotgut
ould make them crazy. If it didn't kill them first.
ither way, I wouldn't think you'd want the Sioux
irred up. There are too many of them, and they take
o the war path at the drop of a hat."

"That's what my father used to say," Nancy said.
He didn't drink much, and he absolutely refused to
rink their whiskey."

"Nancy, you aren't telling me these men carried
our father away just because he wouldn't drink their
whiskey?"

Nancy got up then and went over to the stove. She
athered up her skirt to use as a pad to allow her to
ft the coffee pot from the stove. The action exposed
ne of her legs all the way above her knee, and, for
he first time, Gunn felt a quick awareness of her as a
woman. She seemed oblivious to the fact that she was
iving him a show, or, perhaps she was aware and was
nerely using the pretense of pouring the coffee to
nask it, and thus prolong his look at her legs. She
oured two cups, then brought them back to where
hey had been sitting, and handed one to Gunn.

"You're right," she said. "There is more involved.
Pa has a gold claim that's showing good color. A lot
f the men are jealous at the amount of dust he's

been bringing in. Jealous, or envious, I don't know which. At any rate, I'm sure that had a lot to do with it. Everyone wanted to know where his claim was and he wouldn't tell anyone."

"I'm sure he didn't tell you," Gunn said.

Nancy looked at Gunn with a strange expression on her face. "He didn't tell me," she said. "But how would you know that?"

"It would be safer for you not to know. If you knew, there's a chance someone could get it out of you. If you don't know, they won't even try."

"That's just what Pa said," Nancy said.

"Your pa was right."

"Will you help me, Mister Gunn? Will you help me find my pa?"

Gunn started to say no . . . started to tell her that he didn't make it a habit to get involved in things that were none of his business. But if Hank Meadows was involved, then he had already made it his business. Besides, he couldn't help but think of another young woman at another time. If someone had just come along in time to help, if he hadn't been in town, if the neighbor girl hadn't . . . Gunn let out a long sigh. He wouldn't think of that now.

"All right," he said. "I'll help."

"Oh, Mr. Gunn, thank you!" Nancy said. Spurred by her joy at his agreeing to help, she threw her arms around him and kissed him. At first, she meant it to be a kiss of thanks, of exultation. But the exultation began to turn to excitation, and Nancy began to press her body tightly against Gunn.

Gunn felt the insistent thrust of her breasts, the pressure of her thighs against his, and the heat of her loins, as she pushed against him. He felt himself growing hard, then, just as he was about to give in to the sensations she had given rise to, she pulled away from him.

"Oh," she said. "I'm . . . sorry. I had no right to do that. You must think I'm a terrible wanton."

"No," Gunn said. "I think you are a beautiful woman."

Nancy turned away from him, ashamed to face him with the flush of passion so clearly in her face. "It's just that . . . I'm a woman, Mr. Gunn. I'm a woman with a woman's needs and desires. If we were in a . . . a more civilized part of the world, I could reasonably expect to find a suitable man to marry, and to satisfy those desires. But we are in Deadwood, and most of the men here are not the type I want to associate with. That scarcity of men tends to leave me . . . well . . . unfulfilled. I hope you will forgive me," she said.

"Nothing happened, there's nothing to forgive," Gunn said. He stood up and reached for his coat.

"Oh, are you going?"

"I've got to get a place to stay," Gunn said. "I'll come back to see you tomorrow. We'll get started on tracking down your pa."

"But you don't have to go into town," Nancy said. "You can stay here."

"Do you think that's wise?" Gunn asked.

"I . . . I know what you are thinking," Nancy said, blushing again. "Please stay. I won't make a fool of myself again."

"Nancy," Gunn said softly. "You didn't make a fool of yourself. Honesty is never foolish."

"Then, please stay," Nancy said. She pointed to the

27

sleeping loft. "It's really quite comfortable, and the warmest place in the house."

"All right," Gunn said, smiling at her. "I'll stay."

It was even warmer than Gunn thought it would be, and he lay on top of the mattress with his hands folded behind his head, staring up at the roof. The roof was so low over the sleeping loft that he couldn't stand; in fact, he could barely sit up. The roof was orange, colored by the firelight which escaped through cracks and vents in the stove downstairs.

Gunn had been in bed for nearly an hour when he heard the creaking on the floor. He listened as the creak moved across the floor to the ladder, then he heard each rung of the ladder as it was climbed. He made no sound.

"Mr. Gunn?" It was Nancy's voice, quiet, hesitant. "Mr. Gunn, are you asleep?"

Nancy moved from the ladder to the loft and began crawling toward the mattress. She had put on some perfume. Gunn could smell its note; a scent of lilac, a hint of coriander and something else; a womanly musk which came not from the perfume, but from her own excitement. Gunn felt his pulse increase, his manhood rise.

"Mr. Gunn?" Nancy said again. Now she was right beside him.

"I'm awake," Gunn said.

"I couldn't sleep," Nancy said. "I thought if we . . ." Nancy stuck her hand out to touch him, then was shocked to feel naked flesh. "Oh!" she gasped. She jerked her hand back, but Gunn reached

28

it and brought it back to his body. Her fingers sted on the flat of his stomach. "Mr. Gunn, you . you are naked!" she said.

"Yes."

"Do you always sleep naked?"

"Not always."

Nancy let her hand trail down his stomach, across e wiry bush of hair, then to his manhood which was anding straight up. Slowly, tentatively, she wrapped r fingers around it.

"You knew, didn't you?" she asked. "You knew I ould be up here."

"Let's say that I hoped you would," Gunn said. He ached up to touch her now, and realized that she, o, was naked. His fingers passed across silky nooth skin, traced a path from her shoulder to the rve of a breast, and out to a hard, little nipple. He bbed it gently.

"Ohhh," Nancy said, shivering under his touch. "I ew it would feel like this." She lay down beside m. "Make love to me, Gunn. Show me what it's like be a woman."

Gunn put his arms around Nancy and drew her ose to him. Her lips came to his and he parted them ith his tongue. She didn't retreat from him, but met s tongue with her own in a tangling duet of taste d texture. She was a woman without experience, it not without passion, and she responded to him e a wild animal, writhing, moaning, and flailing r hands about his body. Gunn moved his mouth om her lips and began kissing her on the neck, cking the flesh up into his mouth and biting it.

Nancy increased the tempo of her movements,

29

running her hands up and down his back as if sh
were looking for a hand-hold. Gunn pinched the lob
of her ear gently between his lips, then stuck h
tongue in her ear. He saw her nipple in the sof
orange glow from the firelight, straining as if it we
trying to open, and put her breast in his mouth, the
rubbed her other nipple with the tips of his finger

"Oh," Nancy said, almost whimpering with the jo
of it. "Oh, it's wonderful . . . it's so wonderful."

Nancy saw Gunn move from breast to breast wi
his mouth, then seek out the other parts of her bod
to awaken her to pleasures she had only dreamed o
She lay there, feeling her body being loved, an
watched as the head of her lover moved about on he
arousing her to dizzying heights of sensation. She sa
his head slide down across her stomach, then kiss h
on the inside of each thigh. Her legs trembled unco
trollably. She was in ecstasy, deriving pleasure fro
the slightest touch, or from the brush of his lips, n
matter where they were placed. She was surprised
find that the inside of her legs were as sensitive as h
breasts. She was primed in every fiber of her bein
for sex. Her body longed for it, her mind craved i
and she was about to get that need fulfilled.

Nancy's moans of pleasure turned into cries fo
release. "Oh, Gunn, now, please, now! Don't mak
me wait any longer!"

Gunn felt as if his very blood had turned to boilir
oil. Every inch of his body was sensitized to pleasur
He moved up and spread her legs, then came down o
her, pushing his throbbing cock into the hot w
cavern which was open for him. He came into conta
with her maidenhead, then started to back out.

"No," she said. "No, don't pull back. Do it! Do it!" To emphasize her point, she thrust up against him, and he pushed on through, feeling the tear as it gave way. She gasped and he started again to back out. "No!" she said again, and he felt her hands digging into his back, dislodging pleasure and sending it through the rest of his body, until his whole being was yearning for release.

Suddenly he felt Nancy tense all over. "Oh!" she said. "Oh, what's happening? What's happening . . . oh . . . oh . . . oh!" Each spasm of her climax brought the word out in little barks of pleasure as, with big sporadic jerks, she gave herself over to the release she had attained.

Gunn couldn't hold back any longer, and he felt himself escaping through the part of him that was joined with Nancy. For a fleeting instant, he tried to hold back, then he gave up, and with a final thrust, purged his body of the escaping energy. He could feel the extreme sensitivity of Nancy's breasts, and the completeness of the pleasure Nancy had just attained.

After a few moments, Nancy's hands began roaming again. They found Gunn, now in a flaccid state, and with a few expert strokes, soon had him erect again. The second time they made love she knew what to expect, and they weren't quite as hungry. Gunn was able to coast up to the edge of a climax, then revel in the delightful sensations, and back away from it without going over the edge. They kept this up for a long time, slow pleasurable strokes, exchanged kisses, and the sensitized contact of naked skin against naked skin.

Nancy didn't bother to climb back down the ladder to her own bed. Instead she nestled in Gunn's arms and slept the peaceful, dreamless sleep of one who has tasted total pleasure.

Chapter Three

In the deepest sleep, just before dawn, Gunn was aware of the woman beside him. But he was dreaming, and in his dream, the woman beside him was Laurie.

"Laurie, it's you? But . . . how could it be?"

"I'm your wife, Billy. Did you think I would ever leave you? I love you."

"Yes, but . . ."

"Did you say something, Gunn?" Not Billy, Gunn.

With the intrusion of the third voice, the image of Laurie began to slide out of focus, then break up and drift away. Gunn tried to reach for her, but she was no longer there. Now, like a cork surfacing from deep under water, he began floating back to consciousness.

"No, don't go," he said, and his voice came back to him loud and flat. He opened his eyes and saw the low roof right over his head, and realized that he was in a sleeping loft. Beside him in the bed was a naked woman. She was a pretty naked woman, but it wasn't Laurie. Then he remembered that it was Nancy.

"You were talking in your sleep," Nancy said. Nancy was leaning on one elbow, looking down at him. That action caused her breasts to swing like pendulums, and a nipple trailed across the muscle on Gunn's forearm.

"Did I say anything?"

"A woman's name."

"What was the name?"

"It wasn't mine," Nancy said. She smiled, then sat up and reached for a blanket. "The fire's out and it's cold. I'll get another one started and put on some coffee. What would you like for breakfast?"

"I'll eat breakfast in town," Gunn said, reaching for his trousers.

"That's not necessary. I'll be glad to . . ."

"It would be better," Gunn interrupted. "If I'm going to find your pa, I'm going to have to circulate around. If I get a lead, I'll come back for you and we'll check it out."

"Yes," Nancy agreed. "I guess that's so."

It was true, but that wasn't the only reason Gunn didn't want to eat breakfast there. Since his wife's death, Gunn had set very careful limits on the degree of his involvement with women. He would sleep with them, he would help them when they were in trouble, but he would never take the first step down a path which might ultimately lead to commitment. He had commited himself to Laurie, body and soul, and what had that done for her? Laurie was dead. He had promised to love and protect her, but she was dead. Gunn knew that he could never again afford to give himself body and soul to a woman.

"I'll have the coffee ready by the time you're

34

dressed," Nancy said. "You will at least drink a cup of coffee, won't you?"

"Yes," Gunn said. He smiled at her, and his smile softened his refusal to eat breakfast. "I'll drink a cup of coffee with you."

There were three men in the livery stable. One was small with weasel eyes, and he took out a plug of chewing tobacco, then looked over toward the biggest of the three. "He ain't in the hotel, Meadows. How do you know he's still in town?"

" 'Cause that's his horse," Meadows said, pointing to Esquire. "He ain't gonna be leavin' town without his horse."

The three men in the livery stable were Hank Meadows, and two of his friends. The small one with the weasel eyes was Carl Spenser. The other one was tall, with a handlebar moustache, and he was known only as Sorghum. The three men had been in the livery stable since just before sunrise, and now the snow-covered peaks of the black hills were washed in a red glow as the sun lifted full disc above the horizon. Meadows walked over to stand at the open top of the dutch door so he could look out over the quiet town. Carl was carving off a piece of chewing tobacco of the plug he had pulled out, and Sorghum was stretched out on the barn floor, with his head on a sack of grain and his hat pulled down over his eyes.

"Seems to me like killin' the fella is a long way to go just to get back at him for whuppin' you," Sorghum said from under his hat.

Meadows turned away from the open window and

glared at Sorghum. Both Meadows's eyes were black and his nose was so badly misshapen that it looked as if someone had just placed a large glob of discolored clay on his face. His lower lip was fat, and rolled out, displaying a wicked scar where his lip had been driven into his teeth.

"Maybe you want to face everyone in town today looking like your face just went through a sausage grinder?" Meadows growled.

"Don't get sore at me, Meadows, I didn't have nothin' to do with it," Sorghum replied. "Besides, I'm here to help you, ain't I? Me'n Carl's both here."

"Yeah," Carl said. He slid the chunk of tobacco in his mouth and began chewing. "But I wish the fella would show up. I'm beginnin' to get a little hungry. I'd like to walk over to Kate's Place and see what she's servin' for breakfast."

"You're always hungry, or sleepy, or thirsty, or gotta piss or somethin'," Meadows said. "You'd bitch if they hung you with a new rope."

"I seen Three Finger Charlie Sinclair hung with a new rope," Sorghum said. Sorghum stood up then, and dusted himself off. "He didn't bitch about it, he didn't do nothin', 'ceptin' maybe twitch a little."

Carl Spenser shuddered. "Don't talk like that," he said. "I don't like to hear that kind'a talk."

"Skkkhhhcth!" Sorghum teased, and he held his fist alongside his neck, then tilted his head and ran his tongue out in a mockery of someone being hanged. He laughed at his own impression.

"I said I don't like that kind'a talk!" Carl said.

"Shhh!" Meadows hissed. "Quiet, I see someone comin'."

Sorghum and Carl walked over to stand by the dutch door window.

Meadows chuckled. "Well, lookee here, lookee here," he said. "Looks like the Venable gal done seduced our man into helpin' her. He's comin' from her house."

"You think he spent the night there?" Carl asked.

" 'Course he spent the night there. We know he wasn't in the hotel."

"I wonder if she give him any?" Carl asked.

"Nah," Sorghum said. "They just sat up all night long 'n played cards. 'Course she give him some. He's prob'ly so pussy whipped this mornin' he don't know whether he's comin' or goin'."

"We gonna shoot 'im, Hank? Or we gonna brace 'im?" Carl asked.

Sorghum raised his pistol. "I say let's just shoot the son of a bitch 'n be done with it," he said.

"No," Meadows said. "I want him to know who it was shot him. I want my ugly face to be the last thing that son of a bitch sees before he dies."

"Hank, I don't know," Sorghum said. "Look at the way he's wearin' his iron. I've seen men wear iron like that before. It almost always means they know what they're doin' with a gun."

"I ain't exactly no virgin at this game," Meadows said. "I think I can beat him."

"You thought you could whup 'im too," Carl said. "But look what happened."

"If you remember, he got in the first blow. He hit me when I wasn't expectin' it," Meadows said. "I never had a chance after that. Anyway, there are three of us. I don't give a damn how fast the son of a bitch

37

is, he can't take all three of us. I say we brace him."

The back door to the livery stable opened suddenly, and all three men turned quickly, pointing their guns at the intruder. It was Harry Weiner, the liveryman, just coming to work. He gasped when he saw three guns leveled at him.

"Goddamnit, Harry, give a fella warnin' 'fore you come up on him like that," Meadows growled.

"What is it?" Harry asked. "What's going on?"

"Just get down out of the way over there," Meadows said. "We're fixin' to brace that son of a bitch who come in on the stage last night."

Harry hurried back to the rear of the stable, then ducked down behind the wall of one of the stalls.

Gunn saw a bird start for the warmth of the barn, then wheel around just before he went inside and fly away. If one hundred people had seen the same thing, it would have meant nothing to them. It was only the one in a hundred, the man who lived his life on the edge so that he was keenly attuned to the slightest nuance who would notice something unusual about the bird's behavior.

Until that moment, Gunn had been thinking about where he would have breakfast, and how he would go about looking for Louis Venable. Now, he perceived that he was in danger, so all his senses were focused on one thing; staying alive. He reached down and loosened his gun in its sheath, then stared at the dark opening above the dutch door of the barn. He saw little wisps of breath-vapor floating out of the barn; two . . . no three wisps. There were three men inside the barn, all standing near the door, all watching him. He stopped.

"I see you brought a couple of friends with you, Meadows," Gunn said.

"Goddamn! How'd he know?" Carl asked.

"It don't matter," Meadows said. "We was gonna brace him anyway." Meadows pushed the door open, then the three of them stepped outside. He was in the middle, Sorghum drifted off to Meadows's right, Carl, his left.

"You goin' somewhere, Mister?" Meadows asked. He grinned evilly.

"I was just goin' to breakfast," Gunn answered. His eyes narrowed, his muscles tensed. He was a coiled spring, ready to snap in an instant.

"You don't need to be worryin' none about that," Meadows said. "You're gonna be eatin' breakfast in hell!"

Meadows started for his gun, but Gunn, who was ready for him, had his own weapon out and blazing before Meadows's gun even cleared leather. An ugly, black hole suddenly appeared in Meadows's forehead, and a spray of pink and yellow-gray brain tissue exploded from a bigger hole in the top of his head.

Sorghum was a little quicker than Carl, and Gunn, whose eyes were seeing, and whose brain was interpreting everything, made the decision to send his next shot toward Sorghum, whom he had already perceived to be the next greatest danger. Gunn's bullet caught Sorghum in the shoulder, knocking him down and sending his gun flying. Carl managed to get off one shot before Gunn turned on him, but Carl's shot whizzed by, not finding a mark. Gunn's bullet caught

Carl in the thigh, and Carl yelled and dropped his gun as he covered the hole with his hands. Gunn aimed at Carl for a second shot, then, slowly, he eased the hammer back down and put the gun in his holster. Sorghum had regained his feet now, and he was holding a hand over his wound. Blood was spilling between his fingers.

"Boys, it seems your friend there made a reservation for breakfast in hell. I didn't care to keep it. If you don't want to join him, I'd suggest you get out of here."

Sorghum started to pick up his gun.

"Uh, uh," Gunn said. "Leave your hardware here."

"You son of a bitch," Sorghum said. "I don't let nobody take my gun."

"I just took it, friend," Gunn said. "Now leave it, or be buried with it."

"Come on, Sorghum," Carl muttered. "Help me on my horse and let's get the hell out of here."

Harry Weiner came out of the barn then, leading two saddled horses. Sorghum took the reins from him, then led them over to Carl, where he helped Carl get mounted.

"I'd advise you boys to get the slugs taken out," Gunn said. "If they stay in there, you could fester up and die."

"Mister," Sorghum said. "I'm gonna remember you."

"I know," Gunn replied. "I left you a calling card."

Sorghum clucked to his horse and he and Carl rode out of town, back toward Nancy's house, then beyond.

Gunn watched them as they started up a hill in the

40

distance, watched them until they became black dots against the distant snow. He looked down at Meadows. Meadows was on his back with his arms spread out. The puddle of blood which had formed under his head was already coagulating in the cold. The cold had also stopped the bleeding rather quickly, so that although there were two holes in his head, there wasn't an exceptional amount of blood.

Harry Weiner walked over to look down at Hank. He clucked his tongue, quietly.

"Mister, you've done bit off more than you can chew. Wait'll Jake hears about what you done."

"Saddle my horse," Gunn said.

Weiner began saddling Esquire, while Gunn leaned against the corner of one of the stalls and smoked a quirly.

"Who is this man, Jake, you're talking about?" Gunn asked.

"Oh, Jake's pure bad," Weiner said. "He has this town plumb hogtied, and if any man goes against him, well, such a man gets real scarce."

"You mean nobody sees them again?"

"Not ever," Weiner said.

"Interesting," Gunn replied. Gunn flipped the butt of his cigarette outside, watched the little spark glow, then die. When Esquire was saddled, Gunn mounted. "Where's a good place for breakfast?" he asked.

"You might try Kate's Place, just down the street," Weiner suggested. "She's an old widow woman, come here last year 'n started sellin' homemade pies. Next thing you know she was opening up a cafe. Doin' real good with it too, from what I hear."

There were four men in the cafe when Gunn

41

stepped inside. They were sitting around a table in the back, laughing and talking among themselves, totally oblivious to Gunn's entrance. All of them were wearing work clothes, and none of them were armed. They were the bread and butter of any community, the men who forged the nation's expansion into the wilderness. Weiner had said that the man named Jake had this town hogtied, but Gunn could almost believe that none of these men had even heard of Jake. For a fleeting moment, Gunn wished that he could sit down at the table with them, not for a visit, but as one of them. He wished he was coming into town from his ranch as Billy Gunnison, bound on an errand of commerce, not as Gunn, on some mission of death. He thought of his wife and the supper she would have ready for him when he returned home from a day's work. Then he remembered finding her naked on the bed. Blood was everywhere. The white linen sheets were soaked with it, her pale flesh was smeared with it. And he knew that he could never be Billy Gunnison again.

"Just have a seat anywhere you like, Mister," a woman's voice called from the kitchen. "I'll be right with you."

Gunn sat near the wall so he could keep his eyes on the door and windows. A moment later a heavy-set woman came out of the kitchen. She smelled of flour and cinnamon and apple, and she smiled broadly as she approached Gunn's table.

"What's for breakfast?" Gunn asked. He looked at the woman for a moment, and suddenly recalled another time, another place, when he and half a dozen of his friends had sat around eating sinkers

42

and drinking apple-jack.

"Flapjacks, eggs, potatoes, bacon, sausage. I got some biscuits just took out of the oven. I could fix you up some gravy," the woman said.

"Sausage, biscuits, gravy," Gunn said. "You wouldn't have any sinkers back there, would you?"

"You mean doughnuts?" the woman asked.

"Have you gone fancy, Kate? Sergeant Collins always called them sinkers."

The woman stared at Gunn for a long moment, then she put her hand to her heart and took a step back. She let out a long, low sigh. "Captain Gunnison," she said. "Is it really you?"

"Yes, ma'am, it is," Gunn said. He smiled at the big woman. "How are you doin', Kate?"

"Well, I'm . . . I'm doin' just fine," she said. She took in the cafe with a wave of her hand. " 'Course I don't know what Jeremy would've said about this, but, well, I'm doin' just fine."

"I'm sure Sergeant Collins would have been proud of you," Gunn said. "He always did say you were the best cook west of the Alleghenies, and the few times I got to taste your cooking, I was convinced he was right."

Kate laughed, a loud guffaw. "I'd say he did set a store by my cookin'," she said. "It's a lead pipe cinch he never married me for my pretty looks." Kate wiped a tear, formed perhaps by her laughter, but from a degree of poignancy as well. "I miss him, Captain Gunnison. It's been a long time, but still I miss him an awful lot. One of these days I'm going to take me a trip to this Missionary Ridge place, and I'm going to see just where he did such a fool thing to get hisself killed, and earn that Congressional Medal of Honor I've got in a box in my bedroom."

"He saved a lot of lives, Kate," Gunn said. "Mine included. That medal is well earned."

"It may be, Captain, but it sure can't keep me warm at night." Suddenly she laughed again, and the spell was broken. "Lands, listen to me. You're sittin' there starvin' to death and I'm prattlin' on like a woman gone mad. Let me see to your breakfast."

"Can you set with me a spell?" Gunn asked.

"I'd be pleased to," Kate answered.

Gunn ate heartily while Kate sat across the table from him, drinking coffee. They talked a little about old times, Gunn filled her in briefly on his own marriage, and the fact that his wife was now dead. He purposely skimped on the details. Soon he got around to asking questions about the town. He figured she would be as good a source of information as anyone, and he knew he could trust her.

"It's an evil bunch of men if you ask me," Kate said. "The rotgut whiskey they're dealing in is just half of it. I've got no proof, of course, but I believe they are preying on the miners, and blamin' it on the Indians. You see, they're tryin' to keep the Indians stirred up, 'cause as long as there's trouble between the white man and the Indians, that leaves them free to roam around, doin' near' 'bout anything they want. If you want to find them, you're going to have to go out into the Black Hills and look for them."

"Thanks, Kate," Gunn said.

"Are you going out there?"

"I reckon so."

Kate put her hand on Gunn's arm. "Be careful, will

44

you, Captain Gunnison? Jeremy always did set a great store by you. He said you was the only officer in the entire Union Army worth a bootful of piss."

Gunn laughed. "Thanks, I think."

Gunn finished his breakfast, then gave Kate a big hug. He left the cafe and stepped out to the hitching rail to untie Esquire. That was when he saw Nancy.

"I heard there was a shooting," she said. "I was worried."

"You needn't have been," Gunn answered. He didn't like to have people worried about him; that was one of the reasons for staying a loner. Gunn swung onto his horse. "I'm going out into the Black Hills."

"I'm coming with you."

"Thought you might. We better stop at the livery and get a little feed to take with us. With all the snow, it'll be hard for the horses to graze."

"All right," Nancy agreed.

They rode back down the street to the livery, where Gunn ordered a couple of sacks of oats. While Weiner went inside to get the feed, Gunn lifted Esquire's right forefoot and looked at it. He had noticed a slight favoring of the foot, and now he saw why. There was a rock caught just under the shoe. He picked it out. He saw a man crossing the street from the saloon, coming toward him, and he recognized him as Alves, the saloon keeper.

"Mister, you got yourself two kinds of trouble," Alves said. "That orphan kid, for one." Alves pointed to Nancy. "And Meadows's friends for another. Both will get you killed."

"You one of these friends?"

"Maybe."

45

Gunn stepped away from Esquire and let his arms hang down by his side. He looked at Alves.

"You want to open the ball?" he asked calmly.

"I might," Alves answered. "Meadows was fast damn fast. If you shot him, then it had to be in the back."

"Have you seen the body yet?" Gunn asked.

"No. It's already been took down to O'Dell's. I only just heard about it."

"I shot him. Right here." Gunn pointed to a spot in the middle of his forehead.

Weiner was just coming back from the interior of the barn, carrying the feed Gunn had ordered. He heard the conversation, and he put the bags of feed down.

"That's right," Weiner said. "Hank started drawing first. I never seed anything so blamed fast as this feller's Colt. Was like a whipsnake, just a blur."

Alves raised his hand to his chin and looked at Gunn. "What did you say your name was, Mister?" he asked.

"They call me Gunn."

"Gunn!" The man gasped. He took a couple of steps back, then held his hands out in front of him. "Gunn, I'm not going to draw," he said. "I was just givin' you some advice, tryin' to be helpful. I didn't mean I was goin' to do anything."

"I'm relieved," Gunn said.

"I, uh, have to get back." He pointed to the saloon. "It's nearly time to open. I got some customers like to come in early."

Alves turned and nearly ran back across the street to the saloon. Gunn threw the bags of oats across the

46

saddlehorn, then mounted. "Let's get going," he said.

"Gunn, why was he so frightened when he heard your name?" Nancy asked, puzzled by what she had seen.

"Damned if I know," Gunn answered.

Chapter Four

Earlier that same morning, before the sun had risen, it snowed in the sacred Paha Sapa, the Black Hills. The snow fell heavily, in large, white flakes which drifted down from the black sky and added inches to that which was already on the ground. It fell silently, and its presence deadened all sound, so that the movement of horses, and the stirrings of the Indians in their blankets, were unheard.

It wasn't a village, it was a hunting camp, but all the hunters had left in the middle of the night, leaving only women and children and a few men who were too old or too lame to go on the hunt. There were six tipis in the camp, and there were fifteen Pawnee sleeping in the tipis.

The doors of the tipis were laced tightly shut, and wisps of blue smoke curled up from the smoke flaps, providing a scene of peaceful tranquility to the camp. The smell of half a dozen simmering stews told the silent story of a night when no one went hungry, and when everyone was warm and snug against the elements.

Two hundred yards away from the village lay the lower reaches of a great pine forest, and from the darkness of those trees came shadows emerging from shadows, a dozen riders moving in line. The horses moved silently, as if treading on air, and only their movement and the blue vapor of their breath, gave an indication of life.

A small, chinking sound of metal on metal came from the riders, a sound which was unnatural to the drift of snow and the soft whisper of trees. In the camp a young woman, Smoke Eyes, heard it while in the deepest recesses of her sleep, and her eyes came open and she lay in the darkness and wondered what could have caused the sound. But the bed robes were too warm, and the comfort too sweet, and Smoke Eyes thought she must have dreamed the unusual sound, so she closed her eyes and tried to go back to sleep.

In the tipi with her was her sister, her sister's baby, and the mother of her sister's husband. Smoke Eyes could hear their soft, easy breathing. In the middle of the tipi she saw the dim glow of embers from last night's fire. The embers were still giving off some heat, but very little light. The inside of the tipi smelled comfortably of cooked meat and burning wood, and the lingering musk of love-making from her sister's goodbye to her husband on the night before.

Smoke Eyes recalled lying in her robes and listening to the quiet sounds, her sister's moans of pleasure, her brother-in-law's gasps, the soft, slurping sounds of flesh against flesh. She remembered the strange tinglings the sounds had caused in her own body, and she wondered about the mystery of such things. Soon, she knew that she, too, would be ready to take a husband, and then the mystery would be revealed.

Now, she wished she hadn't thought of that. It seemed that she thought of such things too much lately, and she knew it couldn't be good for her. Finally, she decided that she would get up, leave the tipi to get wood, and return to build the fire. That would keep her busy, and drive such thoughts from her mind. She slipped out of bed, put on shoes, then wrapped a buffalo robe around her naked body, opened the tipi flap and stepped out into the cold, dark morning, to find wood for the fire.

A big, gray haired man sat in the saddle and looked toward the sleeping Indian camp which lay before him. His hair had once been red, and his skin was of the complexion of many red-haired people, fair and freckled. There was a scar on his chin, and he sat fingering it as he looked down on the little camp. It was still an hour before dawn. He twisted around in his saddle and looked over the men who were with him. He was angry that Meadows, Sorghum and Carl weren't here. No matter, he had enough men to do the job, and he would settle with them later.

"O'Toole, are you sure the hunters are all gone?" a man named Taylor asked. Even though he spoke softly, the words seemed to echo loudly in the quiet of the woods.

"Aye," the big man answered. "The red devils left at midnight." O'Toole pulled the cork from a flat whiskey flask, and took several swallows. He handed the flask over.

"What is this?"

O'Toole laughed. "Don't ye be worryin' now," he

said. "Would Jacob O'Toole be givin' his friend the same swill he sells?"

"God, I hope not," Taylor said. He took several swallows of the whiskey, then handed it back to O'Toole. O'Toole corked the bottle then put it away. Suddenly there was a commotion nearby, and O'Toole looked around angrily.

"Would you be keepin' it quiet!" he demanded. "Sure'n we could've brought us a brass band if we were of a mind to make such noise."

"We got somethin', O'Toole," one of the men said. "We found us a squaw woman, gatherin' firewood."

"Did you now? Well, bring her to me."

Two men brought a young Indian woman over to stand in front of O'Toole. She was struggling hard to get out of their grasp, but she wasn't making any noise. O'Toole rubbed his chin and looked at her.

"Tell me, lass. Would you be speakin' English, now?"

"I speak English, O'Toole," the Indian girl said.

"O'Toole is it? And so you know my name."

"I know you. You are the whiskey trader."

"Aye, so I am," O'Toole said. "But you have the advantage of me, lass. Would you be kind enough to grace us with your name?"

"I am called Smoke Eyes."

"Smoke Eyes, is it?" O'Toole said. He stared at the girl's eyes and saw that, rather than the brown which was commonplace for Indians, her eyes were smoky gray. He chuckled. "And so they are, so they are. There's been a paleface in her mother's robes, I can tell you that, laddies," he said.

Those with him laughed.

"Tell me, Smoke Eyes. Would there, perchance, be any warriors in camp?"

"There are many warriors," Smoke Eyes said. "And many other camps like this, close by."

"You know what I think, O'Toole?" Taylor asked. "I think this little lady is giving us some bullshit."

"No bullshit," Smoke Eyes said. "Many warriors. If you shoot gun, they will catch you."

O'Toole held his hand out and made it quiver. "Oh, lass, hush now. Look how it is that you're frightenin' poor O'Toole," he mocked.

"Hey, O'Toole, look at this," one of the men said. He put his hand on the buffalo robe Smoke Eyes was wearing, and pulled it open. Beneath the robe Smoke Eyes proved to be young, beautiful, and naked. There was a quick intake of breath from the men who were close enough to see her.

"Faith, and would you look at that?" O'Toole said. He sighed. " 'Tis a painful duty to be sayin' this, lads, but I want you to cover the lass up."

"Why? She ain't hard to look at," Taylor said.

" 'Tis for that selfsame reason I want her covered," O'Toole said. "Naked beauty like that is likely to be distractin', and we can't afford distractions. We've work to be doin'."

"Yeah, you're right," Taylor said. He looked at the two men who were holding her. "All right, cover her up."

Perhaps it was because they were wanting to take one last look, or, maybe it was because they had a momentary distraction, the very thing O'Toole feared, but, for whatever reason, the girl suddenly managed to slip from the grasp of the two men who

ad her. She did it by the simple expedient of pulling
ut of the robe, leaving them to hold her coat while
he starting dashing, naked, across the snow.

"She knows my name! Don't be lettin' her get
way! Shoot her!"

Taylor drew his rifle from the saddle scabbard,
imed and fired. The girl gave a shout of pain, then
itched forward into a line of bushes.

"I'd better check her out," Taylor said.

"No time to worry about her now. 'Tis the camp
e've got to take care of," O'Toole shouted. "Fire
way, lads! Fire away!"

A woman from the closest tipi had heard the shot
which was fired at Smoke Eyes, and she stuck her
ead out to see what was going on. Someone shot her
nd she fell forward, spraying the white snow with red
lood. After that, an explosion of sound invaded the
eaceful silence as voices shouted in fear and anger,
uns fired, and horses neighed.

The savage butchery started. O'Toole's men shot,
lubbed, or slashed with Bowie knives at the Indian
omen who were running before them. Mothers were
urdered without mercy and children and babies
ere run down and trampled. Old men were shot as
hey tried to mount a feeble defense. It was a gro-
esque montage of sound and fury, savagery and
olor; red blood, white snow and black hearts.

Gunn guided Esquire around a rock, hoping that
he animal would be sure-footed enough to stick to
he trail. He didn't particularly like riding in this kind
f terrain when the ground was covered by snow.

Under snow everything looked the same, and a crum bled ledge, a pile of loose rocks, an exposed root anything that could trip a horse and rider, could als be hidden by the mantle of white.

"Do you have any idea where you're going?" Nanc asked. She was riding behind Gunn, and her horse a least had the advantage of walking through snov broken by Esquire.

"No."

"Then how will you know when you get there?'

"That's a good question," Gunn said.

"If you ask me," Nancy started, but Gunn suddenl held his hand up in warning, and she stopped in mid sentence. They stopped, and were quiet for a lon moment. "What is it?" Nancy asked, quietly.

"I'm not sure," Gunn said. He had seen somethin move where there shouldn't have been movement Now he studied the area closely, trying to pick out th movement again, but all he saw was the white glare o snow. Then, near the rock, he saw it again. He put hi hand over his eyes to shield against the glare an studied the rock closely. That was when he saw th person lying there. He could tell immediately tha whoever it was represented no danger to them. On th contrary, whoever it was seemed to be in danger Gunn got down from his horse. The rock was upslop from the trail, and he didn't want to try and forc Esquire to climb it. He gave Esquire's reins to Nancy

"You stay here. I'm going up there."

"Gunn, what if it's a trap? What if it's a trick someone just waiting to shoot you?"

"I don't think it is," Gunn said. "But if it is, I'll jus have to take that chance."

"What about me?"

"If I'm shot, get out of here," Gunn said.

Gunn started climbing up the slope, slipping on the snow, grabbing handholds when and where he could, falling to his knees a couple of times, until finally he was there. He saw someone lying near the rock, covered with a buffalo robe. He slipped the tie off his gun, just to be cautious, then went up the rest of the way.

Suddenly the person threw off the buffalo robe and stood up, brandishing a knife! It was a beautiful Indian girl, and she was naked. She also had a shoulder wound.

"Well, I'll be damned!" Gunn said.

The girl lunged for him, but Gunn stepped out of her way. She recovered quickly, then her eyes went glassy, and Gunn knew she was about to faint. He tried to reach for her, but with her last conscious effort, she slashed at him, so he couldn't grab her in time to prevent her from falling. She passed out, right in front of him.

Gunn put her knife in his belt, then wrapped her nude body in the buffalo robe, and worked his way back down the side of the hill. It was a little easier coming back than it had been going up, and on the occasion when he slipped and fell, he just sat down and slid a few feet. Finally he was back to the trail.

"Who is that?" Nancy asked.

"I don't know," Gunn said. "It's an Indian girl . . . she's been hurt, that's all I know." Gunn laid her on the trail and Nancy went over to look at her. The robe had slipped open a little, and a breast peeked out, the nipple drawn taut in the cold.

"My God, she's naked!" Nancy said.

"Yes," Gunn answered, smiling. "I noticed that."

"What are we going to do with her?"

"We can't leave her here," Gunn said. He got his canteen and went back over to the girl, then held it to her lips. She felt the water, then reached up and turned the canteen up and began to drink. She opened her eyes then, and Gunn had the strangest feeling that his own eyes were staring back at him. They were the same color as his own. The girl jerked back in fear.

"She's afraid of us," Nancy said.

Upon hearing a woman's voice, the Indian girl showed somewhat less fear. She looked at Gunn and Nancy with more curiosity than fright.

"I am not afraid," the girl said.

"Good," Gunn said. "Because there's nothing to fear. We want to help you. My name is Gunn. This is Nancy. Who are you?"

"I am Smoke Eyes. Are you with the whiskey trader?" she asked.

"The whiskey trader?"

"His name is O'Toole. Jake O'Toole."

"No," Gunn said. "We aren't with him."

"He did this to me," Smoke Eyes said, pointing to the wound on her shoulder. The bullet had only creased her, and though it had been painful, and left a scar, it wasn't serious. The cold had already started the healing. "He also killed many people in my camp. He came with ten riders, early this morning. Our men were on a hunt, there was no one in the camp but women and children. O'Toole shot them all. After all were shot, he burned the tipis. After the tipis were all

56

burned, he left. I watched from the trees. They thought I was dead too. It was very cold . . . I had no coat, no clothes. When O'Toole's men were gone, I went back for my robe. I went to the camp to see if anyone was still alive, but they were all dead."

"What does O'Toole look like?" Gunn asked.

"He is a big man," Smoke Eyes said. "His hair is white . . . his skin is half white, half red."

"Half white, half red?"

"Like this," Smoke Eyes said. She began making dots on her skin with her finger.

"Freckles!" Nancy said. "Gunn, I know him! I didn't know his name, but he's the leader of the men who took my father!"

"That figures," Gunn said. "Jake O'Toole is the name the marshal whispered to me just before he died. He's also the Jake I was warned about in town."

"We've got to find him," Nancy said. "If we can find him, then we can find my father. I know we can."

"Is your father prisoner?" Smoke Eyes asked.

"Yes," Nancy said, "he is. Oh, Smoke Eyes, have you heard about him?"

"The whiskey traders have a white prisoner," Smoke Eyes said.

"Do you know where he is?"

"He is in the cabin of a man named Penrake."

"My father's partner. He disappeared six months ago."

"Will you take us there, Smoke Eyes?" Gunn asked.

Smoke Eyes looked at the tall white man who had found her, and carried her down the mountain. She knew that he had looked on her naked, but she felt no

57

shame. In fact, she felt a strange warmth, deep inside. Maybe this warmth was part of the mystery she wanted to learn more about men and women. She smiled at him.

"Yes," she said. "I will take you."

"Gunn," Nancy said sharply.

"Yes?"

"Don't you think it would be nice if she had some clothes on?" Nancy had noticed the way Gunn had admired the young Indian girl's naked body. More importantly, she had noticed the way the young Indian girl had looked at Gunn. She was determined to keep the upper hand here.

"I guess so," Gunn said. "How far to your camp, Smoke Eyes? Is it close enough to stop for some clothes for you?"

"No clothes there," Smoke Eyes said. "All burned."

"Nancy, do you have anything else in your saddle bag?"

"I have a pair of pants, a shirt," she said. She walked over to her horse and opened the saddle bag, then threw the items of clothing at Smoke Eyes. "Here, put this on."

"Thank you," Smoke Eyes said. She took off the robe and stood stark naked in front of them.

"Cover yourself!" Nancy said. "Have you no shame?"

"Nancy, it's not like she has a dressing room to go to," Gunn said. "Ease off a bit, will you?"

"Well, you could have the decency not to look," Nancy said, and, with a huff, she turned her back. Gunn fired up a quirly, leaned against Esquire, and watched unabashedly as Smoke Eyes put on Nancy's clothes. Smoke Eyes smiled at her audience.

Taylor got off his horse and walked over to report to O'Toole. O'Toole was standing in a clearing where he had built a campfire. He was holding his hands out over the fire, warming himself.

"So tell me, Taylor, did you find the lass?" O'Toole asked.

"Yes," Taylor answered. He stuck his hands over the fire beside O'Toole's. "You were right, I didn't kill her. I only winged her."

"But you finished the job this time?"

"No."

O'Toole looked at Taylor with an expression of surprise on his face.

"What's this? You're tellin' me on the one hand you found the girl, while on the other you're confessin' that you didn't finish her off? And why would that be?"

"Right now she's with the Venable gal," Taylor said. "And a tall, mean-lookin' man."

"That'd be the one we told you about, O'Toole," Sorghum said. "He's the one gunned down Meadows, and shot up Carl and me."

"Ah, yes, the three musketeers," O'Toole said derisively. "Such a help you've been to me."

"What do we do now?" Taylor asked.

"We could trail him for a while," one of the others suggested. "Get us a place where we got a good line of fire, then take him out with a Winchester."

"If he shoots a Winchester the way he does a pistol, you better get him on the first shot," Sorghum said.

"To hear Sorghum tell it, this fella can't be beat," somebody said.

"If this mornin's to be any example, I'd be for sayin' that Sorghum has every reason to think that," O'Toole said. "Anyway, I'm not for killin' our mysterious friend just yet."

"Why not? He's gonna be trouble."

"You did say he's with the Venable girl, did you not?"

"Yes."

"Ah, then where could they be goin', if not to Venable's secret claim?"

"You think the girl knows?"

"Aye, 'tis that sure I am that I was thinkin' on grabbin' the girl next. But now we're spared the bother. We'll just follow a cautious distance behind, and we'll let them lead us right to the claim."

Taylor smiled. "And once we have the claim, we can kill the old man and the mysterious stranger."

"And have a little fun with the girls," one of the men added.

"Tsk, tsk, tsk," O'Toole said. "Shame be on you, for thinkin' such a thing. Don't you know that with money, you'll not be needin' to force yourself on a girl? Why, you can go to any sportin' house in the territory 'n the soiled doves will be bendin' over backwards to share their beds with you. Bendin' over backwards," he said, and he laughed heartily. "Oh, that's a good one. Yes, indeed, that's a good one."

"Well, if we ain't gonna have no fun with the women, what are we gonna do with 'em?"

"Kill them of course," O'Toole said easily.

Chapter Five

"It is there," Smoke Eyes said, pointing to a little cabin which was nestled under a couple of pine trees. The cabin was a gray smear against the solid white backdrop of the snow-covered mountain. A small, pencil line of smoke curled up from the chimney and heat waves shimmered over the roof. To the left rear of the cabin was a small lean-to.

"Do you think my pa is in there?"

"If he is, he isn't alone," Gunn replied. He pointed to the lean-to behind the cabin. "There are two horses there. My guess is there are at least two guards with him."

"What do we do next?"

"I don't know who is inside, but whoever it is, we've got to get them away from your pa," Gunn explained. "If your pa is in there and we start something, they could kill him."

"How will you get them to come out?" Nancy asked.

"I've got to give them something to come out for."

"Do you have any ideas?"

"Yeah," Gunn said, smiling. "I have an idea. But

I'm going to need some cooperation from you two.

"Anything," Nancy said. "I'll do anything it takes."

"Smoke Eyes? Will you help?" Gunn asked.

"O'Toole is my enemy," Smoke Eyes said resolutely. "I will do what must be done."

"All right, ladies," Gunn said. "Let's do it."

Inside the cabin, a small, bandy-legged man walked over to look through the window. He stared at the white blanket of snow outside, squinting his eyes against the glare. His name was Eddie Kitchen, and he had come west from Baltimore with the U.S. Cavalry two years ago. When gold was discovered in the Black Hills, Eddie deserted the army to get rich. When that wasn't successful, he found that he was wanted man with nowhere to go. He had no choice except to work for someone who wasn't particular about the background of his employees. Jake O'Toole was such a person, so Eddie signed on to work for him.

"You're crazy," Eddie said, turning away from the window. "There ain't nobody out there."

"I tell you, I heard a horse blow," Mitch insisted. Unlike Eddie, Mitch had been born in the west. He was about the same size as Eddie, small and wiry, and had spent more of his days working as a cowboy for twelve dollars a month and found. He killed a man in Dodge City, and ran away to the Dakota Territory where he threw in with O'Toole.

"It could'a been anything, wind in the trees, snow falling, even a woodpecker." Eddie explained. He turned away from the window and looked over to ward Venable. The old man was sitting in a chair with his head lolled over on his shoulder. "Think we ought to tie him up?" Eddie asked.

"What the hell for?" Mitch responded. "The son of a bitch can't walk. Hell, we've given him so much of that rotgut whiskey, it's a wonder we ain't killed him. We've 'bout drove him crazy." Mitch chuckled. "I reckon it is about time we give him another drink, though."

"I guess so," Eddie answered. He giggled. "If you ask me, I think the old son of a bitch is beginnin' to like . . . hey! What the hell?" he suddenly said.

"What?" Mitch asked.

"You're right! There is someone out there. Holy shit! Look at that, would you, Mitch? They're both naked!"

Gunn stood just behind a rock, about fifteen yards from Nancy and Smoke Eyes. The two girls were completely nude, standing together, in full view of the cabin.

"Hello!" Nancy called. "Hello the cabin! Would you help us? Would you please help us?"

The cabin door opened and two men came out.

"Who are you?" one of the men asked.

"Just two women in trouble," Nancy said. "We were set upon by bad men. They took our clothes, but we escaped. Please, let us in, let us get warm."

"Sure, lady," one of the men said. He laughed shrilly. "Sure, we'll warm you up." The two men started toward the girls.

"That's far enough," Gunn said, stepping out from

behind the rock.

"Who the hell are you?"

"A friend of the girls," Gunn said.

"Pull on him, Mitch!" Eddie shouted, pulling his own gun. "He can't get both of . . ."

That was as far as Mitch got before Gunn's bullet smashed into his heart, tearing away a big chunk of it, then blowing out a hole in his back the size of a man's fist.

Mitch was surprisingly fast, but, fortunately, not too accurate. Mitch had his gun out and one round fired before Gunn turned to him. Mitch fired a second shot just as Gunn's bullet slammed into his throat and passed through to break his neck. Neither of Mitch's shots found their mark and he was dead before he could fire a third.

"Pa!" Nancy shouted, starting for the cabin.

"Wait!" Gunn called. "Let me make certain there's no one else."

Gunn ran to the corner of the house, pressed his back up against the wall, then eased around to the door. He stopped just outside the door, took a deep breath, then threw himself inside, landing on the ground and rolling across the floor before coming back up in a crouch, ready to fire.

"Shoot me! Go ahead and shoot me! I'll never tell! I'll never tell!" the old man in the chair shouted. His eyes were wide and glazed, and a line of drool fell from his mouth. He was a wild-looking man, but Gunn saw at once that he represented no danger.

"Are you Louis Venable?" he asked.

"Shoot me!" the man said. "Go ahead and shoot me!"

64

Gunn took a quick look around the cabin, saw that it was empty, then stepped to the front door and beckoned for the girls to come in. The girls, clutching their clothes in their hands, dashed naked across the snow to the cabin.

"Pa!" Nancy shouted, when she saw her father. Without bothering to get dressed, she ran to him. "Pa, are you all right!"

"Who are you?" Venable asked. "Why have you come here? I won't tell you where my claim is. Shoot me, I won't tell you."

"My God!" Nancy gasped, and her eyes flooded with tears. "He . . . he doesn't even know me! He's gone mad!"

"It's the whiskey," Gunn said. "Once it's out of his system, he'll know who you are."

Smoke Eyes was dressed by now, and Nancy, as if just noticing that she was the only naked person in the room, moved over to stand by the stove and put her own clothes back on.

"I'm going to go put our horses in the lean-to," he said. "I'll be right back."

Gunn went outside to move the horses. He was concerned about the horses, and he did want to get them into the lean-to. But that wasn't the only reason he went outside. He had noticed earlier that they were being followed, and he wanted to see how close their followers were. Before he returned to the cabin, he slipped his Winchester, and Mitch and Eddie's Winchesters out of the saddle sheaths.

When Gunn returned to the cabin he leaned the three rifles against the front wall, then dropped the bar across the front door. He pulled the shades on the front and side windows, then moved over to one of them to look out.

"What are you doing?" Nancy asked from behind the stove. "Aren't we going to leave? Aren't we going to take Pa back to Deadwood?"

"We'd be shot down before we got a quarter of a mile," Gunn said.

"Shot down? By whom?"

"I imagine it's O'Toole and his men," Gunn said. "I figure that's who's following us."

Nancy was dressed now, and she moved quickly to the window, still tucking her shirttail into her pants.

"Someone's been following us?"

"Yes," Gunn said. "They've been very careful about it, tried to stay out of sight. I picked them up about an hour ago. They're out there now."

"What are we going to do?"

"The next move is up to them," Gunn answered. "They have the cabin surrounded, and they're holding all the cards."

"We're all in position, Jake," Taylor said, reporting to the big, gray-headed man.

"Would you be showin' me where you have the men placed?"

"I've got two on the east side of the cabin, behind those rocks, you see? They're only about seventy-five yards from the window. Anyone who sticks their head in that window can be picked off. There's no back opening to the cabin, but I've got one man back there, anyway. There are two more over on the west side, and the rest of us have the front covered. There's no way anyone inside can get away."

"Nor can we get inside without stormin' the cabin," O'Toole said. "And I've no taste for that, I'm tellin' you."

"You have to give that fella inside credit," Taylor said. "He pulled Mitch and Eddie outta there slick as a whistle with that trick of standin' a couple of naked women out front."

"Aye. Our two lads came out with their peckers in their hands, when they should've had guns," O'Toole said. "I'd give a piece of the old sod to find out who that fellow is in there."

"I don't know who he is," Taylor said. "But to hear Sorghum tell it, he's as fast as lightnin'."

O'Toole took a deep breath, then stood up.

"Hello, the cabin!" he shouted. "Would you be for talkin' a little?"

"I'm not much for talkin'," Gunn answered.

"Sure'n, there's always room for a little talk," O'Toole said. "Talkin' might save a little bloodshed." O'Toole held his hands up, over his head. "I'm comin' in," he said. He started walking toward the cabin. When he was half way there, Gunn called out to him.

"That's far enough."

"Sure'n I'm awfully exposed right here," O'Toole said.

"That's just the way I like it," Gunn said. "Slip your pistol out of your holster."

"But I came to talk," O'Toole protested.

"Slip it out, or I'll shoot it off," Gunn said. "Take it out easy. Use two fingers on the butt."

O'Toole pulled his pistol out of his holster, then stood there holding it between two fingers.

"Now what?"

"Throw it toward the cabin," Gunn said.

"Have you no sense of fair play about you then, man?" O'Toole asked.

"Do it." Gunn's voice was cold, unemotional, and serious.

O'Toole sighed, then flipped his gun forward. It landed in the snow, then sank. "It'll be the devil's own time cleaning it," O'Toole complained.

"Talk," Gunn ordered.

"Before we begin, might I inquire the name of the fellow I'm dealing with?"

"Gunn."

O'Toole gasped, then smiled. "Gunn is it? Well, now. No wonder you were more than a match for poor old Meadows. Don't you think the Christian thing would've been to tell him who you are? Don't you think he had a right to know who he was goin' against?"

"He braced me, O'Toole, I didn't brace him," Gunn replied. "Besides, the way things are, I figure if he had known who I was he wouldn't have bothered to brace me. He would've just dry-gulched me."

O'Toole laughed heartily. "Aye, lad, 'tis likely you are quite correct on that score. Meadows wasn't above takin' every advantage when he could. That's why he had two of my men with him, poor old soul. He thought he had the cards stacked in his favor as it was."

"That's my way of thinkin' on the matter," Gunn said.

"Well, Mr. William Gunnison," O'Toole said. He chuckled. "Aye, I know you, lad. I make it my business to know about men like you. You've cost me five of my best men. Three you've sent on to their great reward, and two out of action with wounds."

"If they were the best you can come up with, you're in pretty bad shape," Gunn said.

O'Toole laughed again. "Aye, you can say that again, lad. And that brings up the reason for my parlay. I want you workin' for me, Gunn."

"Me, work for you?"

"Sure'n workin' for me is not the best way to put it," O'Toole answered. "I'd say workin' with me is more to the truth of it."

"What makes you think I'd work with you?"

"Well, 'tis true you are a wanted man, is it not? There's paper out on you. Oh, it hasn't made it up here, but it's only a matter of time 'til it does. I figure if you're wanted anyway, you might as well make the best of things."

"And you have the best of things?"

"Aye, lad, that I do," O'Toole boasted. "We can make whiskey for no more'n ten cents a bottle. We're gettin' five bucks a bottle when we sell to white men, ten bucks when we pass it off to the Indians. Since we're keepin' all others' whiskey out of here, that gives us the market all to ourselves."

"Is that all you got goin' for you?" Gunn asked.

"Of course not!" O'Toole said, waxing now to his subject. "We're keepin' the miners and the Indians stirred up against each other. The beauty o' that, you see, is that we can hit the miners, clean out their take, and 'tis the Indians'll be blamed. We hit the Indians, take whatever they have, and 'tis put down as retaliation from the whites."

"What about Venable?"

"Aye, himself," O'Toole said. "Well, now, lad. Could be this'll wind up bein' the best of all. You see, Venable has found a rich strike . . . some say the richest strike ever found in the Black Hills. But 'tis of no use to us if he won't tell us where 'tis."

"So you're trying to make him talk?"

"Him, or his daughter." O'Toole chuckled. " 'Twas a neat trick you pulled, strippin' the daughter 'n the Indian girl to get my men out of the cabin. Aye, sir, there's a place for you if you'd care to pitch in with us. Now, Mr. Gunn, what do you say?"

"I say you'd better sit right there and be comfortable," Gunn said.

O'Toole looked confused. "Sit here? I don't understand. What do you mean?"

"I mean I'm not joining you, and you aren't rejoining your men," Gunn said.

"What?" O'Toole sputtered. "See here, Gunn. I came here under your promise of protection. We met to talk, like two gentlemen."

"Who did you talk to before you massacred the Indians?" Gunn asked.

"That was somethin' entirely different!" O'Toole said. "This is a thing of honor!"

"Yeah," Gunn said. "Well, you can honor me by sitting down."

"But . . ."

"Goddamnit! I said sit down!" Gunn roared, and he jacked a shell into the chamber of his carbine and pointed it at O'Toole.

Quickly, O'Toole plopped himself down in the snow.

70

"Jake! Jake, what is it?" Taylor shouted. "What are you doin' in the snow? Come on back."

"Mr. Taylor, 'tis a blackhearted brigand we're dealin' with here," O'Toole said. "A fellow by the name of Gunn."

"Gunn?"

"Aye, does the name mean anything to you?"

"Yes," Taylor said. "I've heard of him."

"Then do your duty, lad," O'Toole shouted, and he rolled over behind a rock out of line from Gunn's fire.

"Open up on 'em," Taylor shouted. "Start shootin'!" At his command, every rifle around the cabin began firing.

The inside of the cabin was like being inside a hornet's nest, but the angry buzzing sounds weren't hornets, they were bullets, and they could kill. Every window in the cabin was smashed, bullets slammed into the walls, and poked holes in the tin smokestack which rose from the stove. Within moments the cabin was so full of smoke from the stove that everyone was coughing and gasping for breath.

Gunn killed three of O'Toole's men, and when he saw O'Toole trying to crawl back to join the others, he kicked snow up close enough to send O'Toole scampering back to the rock he had found.

"Fergis," Taylor shouted. "Fergis, you still alive?"

"Yeah," Fergis answered. "And I'm gonna stay that way. I don't know what you got in mind, but I don't

71

aim to raise up from here."

"You don't have to," Taylor said. "Crawl on back through the ravine to the horses. There's some dynamite in the saddlebags on my horse. Get about six or eight sticks, then get around behind the house and blow it to hell."

"Yeah!" Fergis said. "Yeah! That's a good idea! I'll do that! There ain't even no windows back there."

Fergis left the firing line which Taylor had established, and ran, crouched over, back down the ravine until he came to the horses the men had ridden up on. True to his word, Taylor had several sticks of dynamite in his saddlebags, and a moment later, Fergis had a bomb of eight sticks rigged. He chuckled as he moved around, keeping himself well under cover from any possible fire from the house. Finally he was in position, and he waited for Taylor's signal.

Taylor saw Fergis coming down the hill from behind the house, so he gave a quick wave.

Gunn saw Taylor's signal, and he wondered what it was. There was no back door, no back windows, no way anyone could rush them from behind. What did Taylor's signal mean?

"Who was he wavin' to?" Nancy asked.

"I don't know," Gunn answered. "Keep an eye off to your left."

"All right," Nancy said.

Gunn had put Venable against the back wall, feeling that was the safest place. Nancy and Smoke Eyes had taken Mitch and Eddie's Winchesters, and though they weren't all that accurate with their shoot-

72

ing, they were at least helping to keep the heads of the men who were shooting at them down. With their heads down, they were less accurate, though the pure volume of fire they were shooting toward the cabin made them effective enough. That was amply illustrated when a stray bullet hit Venable, and he let out a gasp of pain. Nancy heard her father gasp. She saw him holding his hand over his chest, with blood spilling between his fingers.

"Pa!" she shouted, and she dropped her Winchester and ran over to him.

"Nancy?" Venable said, recognizing his daughter for the first time. "Nancy, is that you? What are you doing here?"

"Oh, Gunn, he knows me!" Nancy shouted happily. "He knows who I am!"

At that instant, Gunn heard a thump against the back of the house, right on the opposite side of the wall from Nancy and her father. For a moment he was puzzled as to what it could be, then he thought of the signal he had seen Taylor give. Suddenly the hair on the back of his neck stood on end, and he realized what it was.

"Dynamite!" he shouted. "Get down!"

Gunn had just shouted the words when the charge went off. The concussion of the blast hit him like a fist, slamming him against the front wall then knocking him down. The back wall was smashed in with such force that each log became a cannon ball. The roof caved in, then the two side walls. Smoke filled the air so that Gunn couldn't see three feet in front of him.

As it happened, Gunn and Smoke Eyes were under

an "A" frame, formed by several of the logs from the back wall. That frame sheltered them from the collapse of the roof and the rest of the house, and they escaped with no more than a little concussion. Nancy and her father weren't so lucky. They were crushed by the rear wall.

"Nancy! Nancy!" Gunn called. He crawled over to her then caught his breath sharply. Nancy's eyes were open, but they wore the glassy stare of death. Nancy and her father had both been killed in the blast.

"Are they dead?" Smoke Eyes asked.

"Yes," Gunn replied.

"Are you hurt?" Smoke Eyes asked.

"No. How about you?" Gunn replied.

"I am not hurt," Smoke Eyes said. She crawled over beside him, then sat up and began dusting herself off.

Gunn felt her body against his, but he could not take his gaze off Nancy, the life in her gone—forever.

Chapter Six

Gunn pulled his parka about him more tightly, and, standing in the stirrups of his saddle, looked down on the other side of the mountain. It had been three hours since the shootout at the cabin, and in all that time, Gunn hadn't seen anyone following them. He was convinced now that, for reasons of his own, O'Toole had abandoned the search.

All around them, the world was painted in harsh white and stark black, covered with a blanket of snow. About half a mile below them, on the mountain he and Smoke Eyes had just crossed, he saw a small encampment, consisting of two tipis and a campfire.

They hadn't happened on the encampment by accident. They had smelled the woodsmoke earlier, and merely followed the scent to this point.

"Do you recognize the tipis?" Gunn asked.

"No. They are not of my village."

Gunn leaned forward and patted his horse on the neck. "I hope they are friendly to you."

"They will be friendly to me."

Gunn chuckled. "What I had in mind was, I hope

they are friendly to both of us."

"It will be best if I ride in front," Smoke Eyes offered.

"Not like that, it won't. You're dressed like a white woman," Gunn reminded her. "The way O'Toole's got things stirred up now, it could be dangerous for whites to ride into an Indian camp."

"They will know I am Indian."

The two of them started down the mountain toward the camp below. Gunn could see a woman working around the fire, and a short time later, he saw two more figures in the encampment . . . another woman and a man. He knew also that he and Smoke Eyes had been seen, because their approach was as visible as black ink on white paper. Their horses left trails in the snow behind them, long, dark scars on the face of the white mountain.

"Hello the camp," he called when he was within easy speaking distance.

"I know'd you was a white man from the way you was ridin'," the man at the encampment answered, and his voice confirmed what Gunn had realized for the last several minutes, that the man, at least, was white. "Get down, get down, you're welcome."

"What about your friend in the tipi with the Sharps?" Gunn asked. "Does he welcome me too?"

The white man laughed. "You seen 'im, did you?"

"Not exactly. But there were four horses, two women, and two tipis. When I saw the flap open on one of them, I figured that's where the other one had to be. Is he white, too?"

"Nah, he ain't white. Come on out, Two Eagles," the man said, and the flap opened and a middle-aged

Indian stepped out. The Indian said nothing. He put the big .50 Sharps down, wrapped himself in a robe, then walked over and sat on the ground near the campfire.

"You ever see what a .50 bullet does to a man's flesh?" Gunn asked. "That's a lot of gun."

"Don't have it for shootin' at men," the man said. "Use it for buffalo, 'n ever' now 'n again, a bear. Only had to shoot it at a man once, 'n I fetched him from four hunnert yards away. It tends to keep people away that I want to keep away."

"I can see how it would. I have some coffee," Gunn said, swinging down from his saddle. He opened the saddlebag and took out a pouch.

"Coffee? Damn, it's been week of Sundays since I had any coffee. Kettle Woman, fix us some coffee," he said, handing the pouch to one of the women. Both women were moon faced and plain looking, but they had friendly smiles for Gunn and Smoke Eyes. "We got some good camp stew on. Would you stay a while?"

"I was hoping you would invite us," Gunn said.

"The name's Ebenezer Gilseth, though I answer to Eb. What's your name? That your squaw?" Before Gunn could answer either question, Eb went on. "She's a real pretty one, she is. I had me a pretty one before I got Kettle Woman here. Trouble she know'd she was pretty, 'n ever' time we'd go into a town, why, all the white men would gawk at her. Next thing you know'd they was offerin' her all sorts of geegaws and doodads, and the girl up 'n run off with a drummer. Now Kettle Woman here, she's ugly as a mudhen, 'n she knows it. She knows how lucky she is to have a

77

husband too, so she really treats me right. She works hard an' she's a good cook, 'n she keeps me warm at night. Yes, sir, give me an ugly one ever' time. But I'll say this for your woman. She's a pretty one. Say, you never did tell me your name."

Gunn laughed. "I never got a chance to get a word in edgewise."

Eb laughed with him. "I reckon you didn't," he said. "That's my problem, I don't get no one to talk to out here. Take Two Eagles there, he don't talk no white man talk a'tall, and damn little Indian. Kettle Woman and Quiet Stream . . . Quiet Stream is Two Eagles' woman, they talk some white man talk and a whole lot of Indian. Only trouble is, for all their talkin', they don't talk 'bout nothin' I got a particular interest in. So what is your name?"

"Gunn."

"That's all? Just Gunn?"

"That's all I use."

"Well, it's your moniker. I reckon you can use whatever you want to use."

Eb was a big bear of a man, with a full, bushy black beard, and long, scraggly black hair. Though he, like Two Eagles and the two women, was dressed in buckskins and buffalo robes, the beard had been Gunn's earliest indication that he was approaching the camp of a white man.

The two women had been talking to Smoke Eyes all the while Gunn and Eb had been talking. Kettle Woman suddenly got louder, and started making angry clucking noises. Gunn looked at her in surprise, then saw that Kettle Woman was not angry with Smoke Eyes, but was just angry over whatever Smoke

Eyes was telling her.

"What is it?" Gunn asked. "What's wrong?"

"I told them about the attack on our camp this morning," Smoke Eyes said. "They are saying angry things about O'Toole."

"O'Toole?" Eb snorted. "You ain't no friend of his'n, are you?"

"Hardly," Gunn said. "He just tried to kill us. He did kill two others who were with us . . . a girl named Nancy Venable, and her father, Louis Venable."

"Louis is dead?"

"Did you know him?"

"Not too well," Eb said. "But I have run across him in the hills a few times. I'll say this for him . . . if all the gold hunters were like Louis Venable, there wouldn't be no trouble between the Indians and the white man. He was a good man . . . he had respect for the Indian's sacred grounds."

"What do you know about O'Toole?"

"If you ever heard the term black Irishman, it was O'Toole they were talkin' about," Eb said. "He's been riding through, raising bloody hell with the whites and the Indians. If he don't get stopped pretty soon, he's likely to touch off a war . . . I mean a big war."

"I intend to stop him," Gunn said resolutely. "I owe that to Nancy."

"I hope you do, Gunn, I hope you do," Eb said. He sniffed. "Smells to me like the coffee is about done. What say we have a cup, then a little stew?"

"Sounds good," Gunn said.

"Gunn, you wouldn't have any whiskey on you, would you?" Eb asked, rubbing his chin hopefully. "I don't mean that poison O'Toole's spreadin' around. I mean some real sippin' whiskey."

" 'Fraid not, friend," Gunn said, and he wished then that he did have, for he knew what a comfort a drink could be after a long, dry spell.

Smoke Eyes and the two Indian women chattered all through the meal, while Eb unloaded all the stories he had been saving for the next occasion he had white company. Some of his stories were so funny that he and Gunn laughed until tears came to their eyes, and the women, though they hadn't even heard the stories, were tickled by the men, and they joined in with the laughing.

Some of Eb's stories were anything but funny. He confirmed that there had been at least half a dozen incidents similar to the raid on Smoke Eyes' camp that morning. And O'Toole's violence wasn't limited to Indians. Last spring, Eb said, O'Toole and his men attacked a miners' camp, killed and scalped six men.

"I remember hearing about that incident," Gunn said. "But I thought the miners were killed by renegade Indians."

"Sure, that's what O'Toole wanted ever'one to think," Eb said. "Reason I know different, is they was a huntin' party nearby, 'n when they heard what was goin' on, they rode over to have a look-see. It was too late for them to do anythin' to stop it by the time they got there, 'n anyway it was between whites so they figured it was none of their business. But they saw it, and the word is all over the nations that O'Toole was the one what done it."

"Why hasn't anyone gone to the federal marshal?"

"You think anyone'd take the word of an Indian on somethin' like that?" Eb asked. "Hell, they wouldn't even take my word anymore. I've lived with 'em so long they figure I've become tainted myself."

"I believe you," Gunn said. He finished the stew, then cleaned out his bowl and handed it to Kettle Woman. "An-he," he said. "Very good."

Kettle Woman laughed, and looked toward the ground in embarrassment.

"I got a little terbaccy," Eb offered.

"No, no, save yours," Gunn said. "I'll be getting back into town to get some more. We'll smoke mine."

Gunn rolled a quirly, Eb filled a pipe, and they smoked and talked more. Gunn knew that Eb was enjoying the conversation, but Gunn was profiting from it as well. He was getting information on O'Toole that would be invaluable in his hunt, for, though he had been the hunted today, after today, he intended to become the hunter.

The sun set early, and darkness came quickly. That was when Eb offered his tipi.

"We can't do that," Gunn said. "Where will you and Kettle Woman sleep?"

"We'll sleep in with Two Eagles and Quiet Stream," Eb said. He chuckled. "We do that sometimes, anyway. Kettle Woman likes to hear other people rootin' around in the night. It gets her all hot and bothered, if you know what I mean. 'Course, you not bein' used to that, I reckon you and your woman will want a little privacy."

"She's not my woman," Gunn said.

"Gunn," Smoke Eyes said. "Would you shame me in front of the others?"

"Shame you? No, of course not."

"I have told them I am your woman," Smoke Eyes

81

went on.

"Smoke Eyes, why would you tell such a thing?"

"You saved my life," Smoke Eyes said.

"Yes, but that doesn't make you my woman."

"Do you find me ugly?"

"No, of course not. I think you are very pretty."

"Then, what is the hurt to pretend I am your woman, even if I am not? It will make me look good in their eyes."

"The girl's got a point there, Gunn," Eb said. "Besides, it'll be nice to have something to snuggle up to tonight. It gets awful cold up here after the sun goes down."

"If we share the same robes and blankets, we will sleep warm tonight," Smoke Eyes said. She smiled at him. "I saw the way you looked at me today. I know I was pleasing to you."

Gunn remembered the sight of Smoke Eyes naked, and he felt a sudden heat in his blood, warm enough to cause him to forget the cold which was already beginning to numb the skin.

"Yeah," he said. "You were pleasing to me."

"Your woman speaks real good white talk," Eb said. This time, Gunn didn't even correct him when he called Smoke Eyes his woman.

"I went to school," Smoke Eyes said, smiling proudly. "I know George Washington. He is president."

"He was the president," Gunn said. "Grant is the president now."

"Why is George Washington not president?" Smoke Eyes asked, confused by Gunn's information.

"He's dead."

82

"Oh," Smoke Eyes said. She looked down sadly. "I am sorry to hear this."

"It's all right, the country's got over it," Gunn said. Eb chuckled.

The flames of the fire had died down by now, and only the banked embers provided warmth and light. The five figures around the campfire were orange-lit from the front, and shadowed in the rear. A piece of wood popped, and several glowing ashes rode the rising column of heat lazily up into the night sky, reaching for the star-dust which lighted up the heavens. On the nearby mountain tops large pine trees thrust up as if they were supporting columns for the heavenly display of lights. In the distance, a lonely wolf called for its mate.

Kettle Woman began pulling on Eb. She said something, and everyone, even Two Eagles, laughed. Only Gunn didn't laugh, because he didn't know what she said. Finally, Eb sighed.

"Looks like I ain't gonna get no peace around here 'til I go to bed 'n take care of this fool woman," he said. He pointed to the other tipi. "That one's yours, there's plenty of fur robes and blankets in there. It sleeps real comfortable."

"Thanks," Gunn said. He watched as Eb and Kettle Woman, and Two Eagles and Quiet Stream disappeared into their tipi, then he turned toward Smoke Eyes. She stared at him with her large, gray eyes, then looked down at the ground and smiled.

"What was everyone laughing about?" Gunn asked.

"Kettle Woman," Smoke Eyes said. "She was thinking about you and me together in the blankets and she was, I don't know how to say it, she wanted to . . ."

Gunn chuckled. "You don't have to go on, I get your point," he said. "Well, are we going to stay out here all night?"

"I go first," Smoke Eyes said. "You wait here until I call for you."

"All right," Gunn agreed, smiling at her. "If you've decided to be the shy maiden after all this, it's fine with me."

Gunn watched as Smoke Eyes disappeared into the darkness of the tipi, and he waited outside for her to call. He was the only one left now, and he looked around the silent camp. Esquire and the other horses were tied near a break of trees, dark, unmoving shadows in the night. A wolf called again, and then, much closer, an owl. A coal popped in the fire, and a shower of sparks fountained up, then dropped back down. The popping ignited a small flame which danced for a moment then died into an orange glow once more.

"Gunn?" a soft voice called from inside the tipi.

Gunn stepped into the tipi, then pulled the flap closed behind him. It was pitch dark inside, and he stood still, lest he stumble over her.

"I can't see you," he said quietly.

"I am here," she said, and her voice was very close, and warm and intimate, and he felt his blood run hot.

"Just a minute," he said, and quickly, he undressed in the dark. He could feel the cold night air on his nude body as he stood there, and he felt around with his bare feet until he could feel the buffalo robe which covered the blankets. He dropped down to his knees, then crawled forward, feeling with his hands, until he felt the resilience of soft, smooth, warm flesh, and a hard, tight nipple. With a quick intake of breath he realized he had just felt her breast.

Smoke Eyes lifted the blanket and Gunn moved under it, pressing his nude body against that of the young Indian girl. The heat of their bodies quickly warmed the robes, so that they were oblivious to the cold around them, and cognizant only of the cocoon they shared.

Gunn ran his hands across her body, feeling the delightfully smooth flesh, seeing with his fingers what darkness denied his eyes. His hands moved from her breasts across her flat stomach, and out along the flare of her hips, then across her thighs until they were at her warm, moist cleft. His fingers moved down into the gash, slipped through the hot cream of her juices until they found the quivering little nub of flesh which set Smoke Eyes' body into convulsive chills of pleasure.

Smoke Eyes' own hands were exploring Gunn's body as well, and he felt the delicate brush of her fingers as she touched and explored. Finally her hand wrapped around his penis, and he heard her gasp as she realized what it was.

The moment soon arrived when neither of them could wait any longer, and Gunn rolled onto her, his cock pushing up between her legs until it found the damp, yielding flesh of her sex. Smoke Eyes moaned with pleasure, and though she had never done this before, she raised her legs up intuitively.

"I have heard my sister moan in pleasure," Smoke Eyes gasped. "But I have never known the pleasure she felt until this moment."

85

Gunn was surprised by her statement. She had clearly been the aggressor in this relationship, and yet now he was learning that she was a virgin.

"I am on fire inside," she moaned. "Are you on fire?"

"Yes," Gunn said, and though he had answered just to satisfy her, he realized that he was.

For a moment, Gunn felt a quick sense of betrayal to Nancy. But the sense of betrayal was for a moment only. If he was betraying Nancy now, then he had betrayed Laurie every time he ever made love to a woman, and he knew that wasn't true. He had loved Laurie, as he had never loved another woman, as he knew he could never love another. He had made love to Nancy, but he hadn't loved her. And now he was making love to Smoke Eyes, and though he didn't love her with a love that was permanent, he loved her very deeply right now.

For Gunn, all time was suspended, and, for this moment at least, nothing else existed or mattered. There was no O'Toole, there was no self-imposed mission to find him, there had never been a Nancy. There were only the two of them, alone in the world.

Gunn went to Smoke Eyes tenderly, passionately, rolling onto her to complete what had been started. He felt his cock slip through the swollen outer lips to plunge into the soft, inner heat. He reached the membrane of her maidenhead, confirming the truth of her earlier statement. She felt him stop, and she put her hands behind him and pulled, showing by that action that she wanted all of him. She thrust up against him, just as he went down, and the maidenhead parted, letting him sink deep inside to feel the rush of wet heat against his shaft.

Beneath him, Smoke Eyes shuddered with her first climax, and she heard the sounds coming from her own throat which she used to hear in the night, and now she knew. The mystery had been rolled away, and she knew, and she gloried in the knowledge of it as she felt the spasms of pleasure flooding over her body.

Gunn thrust very deeply, several more times, until he felt his own juices suddenly boil over and shoot out, spraying his pleasure deep inside the lovely young Indian girl beneath him. He felt, for a moment, as if he were melting inside, pouring himself into the girl from the very marrow of his bones. Then, finally, he was through, and as the last spasms of pleasure washed through his own body, he felt the tiny quivers of aftershock which Smoke Eyes was still enjoying. He stayed on top of her for a moment longer, then he rolled off to lie in the robes beside her, as she snuggled against him.

Gunn smiled into the darkness. It was below freezing outside, but he and Smoke Eyes were actually sweating. If there were only some way to save this heat to be used later.

If only there was some way to stop time in its tracks.

Chapter Seven

It was late the next day after the encampment with Eb. The sun was high and bright off the snow as Gunn and Smoke Eyes rode across the folds of hills, one after another. As they crested each ridge, another was exposed, and beyond that, another still. Gunn had used ashes from last night's campfire to place black smudges under his eyes and that helped to reduce the glare. Despite that, the glare was still so intense that, when he saw the wrecked wagon for the first time, he thought it was just another outcropping of rocks, somewhat different from the others. He stared at it more closely.

"Smoke Eyes," he said, pointing to the object which had drawn his attention. "That's a wagon isn't it?"

"Yes," Smoke Eyes said.

"Has it been here long?"

"I have never seen it," Smoke Eyes said.

"Maybe we'd better have a look," Gunn suggested, and he slapped his legs against Esquire to urge the Tennessee Walker into a quick lope.

As they rode toward the wagon, Gunn saw two

clumps of bright color lying in the snow behind the wagon. When he got closer, he realized what he was seeing. He was looking at bodies . . . women's bodies. The bright color he saw was the fabric of their dresses.

Gunn and Smoke Eyes dismounted as they reached the wagon, and Gunn walked over to look down at the bodies. The coyotes had not yet discovered them, for, except for the wounds which killed them, they were unmarked. It was a woman and a little girl, lying side by side in the grass. They had both been killed by gunshot wounds. A short distance beyond the wagon, Gunn saw a man lying on his back. The top of his head was cut away and brains had spilled out into the snow. There were arrows in the man's body. The team which had pulled the wagon was gone, and the wagon itself was wrecked, by having all four wheels smashed. As a result, the bed of the wagon was lying flat in the snow.

Gunn walked over to the man and pulled one of the arrows out and looked at it. "Well, I guess I can't blame the Indians too much," he said. "Women and children were killed in the camp, I guess, in their mind, this evens the score."

"Indians did not do this," Smoke Eyes said.

"Smoke Eyes, you're not responsible for everything any Indian does," Gunn replied.

"White men did this," Smoke Eyes insisted.

"What makes you think so?"

"That is not the way my people take a scalp."

Gunn looked at the man's head and saw that it wasn't a typical scalping job. An Indian took a scalp as precisely as a surgical operation. A slit just above the ears to loosen the scalp, then a peeling. If the victim wasn't already dead, it was possible to survive a scalping, and Gunn knew of cases where people had survived. No one could've survived the butcher who worked on this man.

"I'll agree that I've seen better scalping jobs," Gunn said.

"And the arrow," Smoke Eyes said. "It is Minneconjou, the people who were attacked yesterday were Pawnee. It is not for the Minneconjou to take revenge for the Pawnee."

Gunn walked over to look into the wagon. "I'll be damned," he said. "Smoke Eyes, it looks like you were right," he said. He reached down into the wagon and picked up a box of rifle cartridges. "No Indian raiding party would leave ammunition."

"It was O'Toole," Smoke Eyes said.

"Yeah," Gunn said. "Mr. O'Toole's account just keeps getting bigger. He's going to have quite a bit to settle up with when we meet again."

Gunn saw a little black notebook next to where the cartridges had been, and he picked it up.

MY DIARY
by Mary Conroy

Day One:
Pappa says there are gold nuggets as big as bird's eggs, just clinging to the grass roots in the Black Hills. He says we are going to go there and get just enough gold to get a new start in Oregon. I wonder what lies ahead for us?

The diary was full of girlish dreams and hopes,

including a "secret" poem for her "secret" beau she had to leave in Missouri. Gunn closed the book and put it back down. The little girl's dreams and hopes were finished now. Her childish notions of romance, her self-conscious poem to her secret beau were but unanswered whispers now. She would never marry, have children, grandchildren.

Yes, sir. O'Toole would have a lot of settling up to do.

There was enough canvas from the wagon top to make rough shrouds for the three bodies, so Gunn directed Smoke Eyes to make the shrouds while he dug one common grave for them. Afterward, he and Smoke Eyes stood over the grave for a long, silent moment.

After the impromptu funeral for the Conroy family, Gunn and Smoke Eyes resumed their travel, following the trail left by the horses which had ridden away from the wagon. There had been very little talk before they discovered the wagon, and even less, afterward. When night came, they built a fire, ate a supper of beans and jerky, then lay out their sleeping bags. Smoke Eyes climbed into her sleeping bag, and waited for Gunn to come to her.

Smoke Eyes recalled the long, languorous moments spent making love last night, and she felt a still-lingering sense of pleasure. She felt the heat of desire stirring within her, and she wondered if she dared tease him into making love again.

No, she wouldn't ask him. She would wait for him.

Smoke Eyes thought about Gunn. He wasn't like any of the white men she had ever known before. He wasn't like Mr. Tucker, the Indian agent who was very small and wore glasses which were so thick that his eyes appeared to be very large. He wasn't like Mr. Johnson at the trading post, who was flabby and pale and had no hair and sweated a lot.

Gunn was more like an Indian than a white man. But he was like the lean, handsome Indians who rode on the hunt, not like the ones near the towns who sold firewood from their wagons, and who had fat bellies which hung over their belts.

Smoke Eyes watched glowing sparks from the fire climb high into the sky, there to get lost among the stars. She breathed a prayer into the rising column of smoke and sparks, so that the prayer would be carried quickly to the Wakan who looked over all spirits. If the Wakan agreed that she should be Gunn's woman, Gunn would come to her. If it was not the Wakan's will that she would be Gunn's woman, she would sleep that night undisturbed.

"Smoke Eyes. Smoke Eyes, it's time to break camp."

Smoke Eyes opened her eyes and saw Gunn standing next to her, rolling up his sleeping bag. Without a word, she got up and began rolling up her own bag. He had not come to her during the night. It was not Wakan's will that she be his woman.

Jerky and last night's warmed over coffee served for breakfast, then Gunn and Smoke Eyes were on their way again. They rode in silence for nearly an hour, then it came to Smoke Eyes that she should return to her people.

"Gunn?"

"Yes?"

"Last night, I asked the Wakan to give me a sign."

"What sort of sign?"

"I wanted to know if I would be your woman."

"Smoke Eyes, I don't want to . . ."

"It is all right," Smoke Eyes answered. "I know that I am not to be your woman. This was the sign given to me."

"I'm glad you understand."

"I am going to return to my own people."

"You don't have to. If you want to ride with me, you can," Gunn said.

"No, it is right that I should return to my own people," Smoke Eyes said. "They must be told that the evil things being done by O'Toole are being done to the Indian and white. They must understand that O'Toole is the enemy of all, and that the Indian and white man are not enemies."

"Yes," Gunn said. "It will be good for you to tell them this."

Smoke Eyes held up her hand. "Goodbye, Gunn." She smiled. "When the fires of the camp have burned low and I hear the women whimpering in pleasure because their men have come to them, I will think of you."

O'Toole tied his horse at the hitching rail in front of the post headquarters. Out in the quadrangle a company of soldiers drilled, their breath raising a cloud of vapor as they exercised at the commands of their sergeant. A private and a lieutenant exchanged salutes, and a couple of the women of the post passed through the sallyport from the married officers' quarters, headed for the sutler's store.

O'Toole took it all in and chuckled. He had dealt with the military before. He served first in the Union army during the Civil War, when he was paid by a wealthy draftee who, as was the custom, hired him to serve in his stead. O'Toole deserted, sold his services again and deserted again, and he did it still a third time before he feared he would be recognized. After that he wound up with Quantrill. With Quantrill, however, he learned there were no politics. Though ostensibly riding for the South, O'Toole was in fact, riding for himself, taking whatever he could from anyone he could, regardless of whether they were loyal to the North or South. Quantrill rewarded him not only with his share of the spoils of war, but also with a major's commission. O'Toole still used that title when it suited him to do so, such as now, when dealing with Colonel Proxmire, the commanding officer of Fort Thompson.

O'Toole stepped into the post headquarters building, where he was greeted by the post sergeant-major.

"Yes, sir? May I help you?" the sergeant-major asked, looking up from his desk.

"Aye, my lad, 'n top o' the mornin' to you," O'Toole said. "Would you be so kind as to tell your colonel that Major O'Toole wishes a word with him?"

"Major O'Toole?" the sergeant-major asked, his eyebrows raising in question.

O'Toole chuckled. " 'Course 'tisn't Major O'Toole now, though that was my rank in the late unpleasantness and I fear 'tis stuck with me." Left unstated was the fact that O'Toole's commission came from neither government in the latest "unpleasantness," but from Quantrill.

"I'll tell the colonel you're here, sir," the sergeant-major said.

O'Toole walked over and examined a map on the wall while the sergeant-major conferred with Colonel Proxmire. The route and times of every army patrol were listed on the map, and he smiled as he assimilated the information. This was invaluable knowledge to him for planning his forays against the Indians, and the miners.

Colonel Proxmire appeared in the door of his office.

"Major O'Toole?"

"At your service, sir," O'Toole said.

"Come in, Major O'Toole," the colonel invited, and O'Toole smiled. He had already won his first round, the colonel had accepted his rank without question. "What can I do for you?"

" 'Tisn't what you can do for me, Colonel, but what I might be able to do for you," O'Toole said.

"Oh? And what would that be?" Colonel Proxmire asked.

"Colonel, though I was once a military man like yourself, I'm now a trader of goods."

"A trader?"

"Aye, Colonel, a trader. And my wanderings take me all through the Black Hills where I see all sorts of things. Things you might find useful in your duty."

Colonel Proxmire began filling his pipe, and he looked up at O'Toole.

"Go ahead," he said. "What sort of things?"

"Well, for example, I hear things you understand

95

. . . things from good Indians about bad Indians. Like just the other day, I was told of a bunch of savages who planned to make war against the whites."

"And where are these savages now?"

"All dead, Colonel," O'Toole said.

"Dead?"

"Aye, dead."

"What happened to them?"

" 'Tis proud I am to tell you, Colonel, that my men and I dispatched these heathens to their happy hunting ground."

"Were you attacked by these Indians, Major O'Toole?"

"Attacked? Oh, my, no, no, we weren't attacked, Colonel. 'Twas we who done the attackin'. We discovered their camp early one mornin', and we made quick work of them."

"Major O'Toole, if you are attacked by Indians, you certainly have every right to respond in defense of your own life. But you have no right to attack Indians without provocation."

"Oh, we had provocation enough, sir," O'Toole said. "I've no wish to be takin' on your duty for my own, Colonel, but 'twas no time to send for the army before the savages did their foul deed."

"A foul deed? What foul deed?"

" 'Twas a poor settler and his family," O'Toole said. "We found their wagon wrecked, their team stolen, and the father, mother, and little child butchered by the savages."

"Butchered, you say?"

"Aye. Bodies full of arrows, scalps taken. During the war I saw many sad sights, Colonel, as I am sure did you. But I must confess to being moved near to tears by the plight of this poor, helpless family. Well, sir, 'twas on my way to report to the army, when we happened across the savages who were responsible for the massacre. I beg your forgiveness, sir, if we acted imprudently. But I vowed that I would rather accept the consequences of the act than to allow those savages to breathe one more day while their victims lay so brutally murdered."

Colonel Proxmire had forgotten all about his pipe during O'Toole's telling of the story. Now, remembering again, he tapped the tobacco down and lit it. He took several puffs and was wreathed in smoke before he spoke again.

"Major, when you came in, you said you were going to do something for me. Were you talking about this?"

"Aye, this 'n more," O'Toole said. "Colonel, you run regular patrols through the Black Hills, do you not?"

"Yes."

"Could you be makin' me privy to that information, Colonel? The reason I'm askin' is, I wander through those self-same hills in pursuit of my trade. If I knew where your scouting patrols were at all times, I could better reach you if I had information which would be of use to you."

"Yes," Colonel Proxmire agreed. "Yes, I can see the validity in that. Perhaps if you had known where our patrol was when you were first informed there was a war party about, you could have warned us in time to . . . to prevent the tragedy you saw."

"I'm glad you agree, Colonel," O'Toole said. He

handed a piece of paper to the colonel. "If you could just send the schedule to this address in Deadwood, I'd receive it. That way we could be workin' together to keep peace in these hills, for white and Indian alike."

"Very well, Major O'Toole," Colonel Proxmire said, shaking O'Toole's hand. "I'll be glad to provide you with a schedule of the movements of my men. Please be assured that the United States Army is grateful for any and all information you might be able to provide."

O'Toole rode away from Fort Thompson, chuckling over what he had just accomplished. With the patrol schedule, he had nothing to fear from the army. As long as he knew where the soldiers were, he would be able to avoid them. All he had to do now was take care of Gunn.

He had let it be known that he would pay a fifteen hundred dollar reward for Gunn, not dead or alive . . . just dead.

Stone dead.

Chapter Eight

Sorghum was sitting at a table with Buck Pied-mont, Alan Chewpack and Earl Spaulding in a saloon in Mystic, a town about twenty-five miles south of Deadwood. Mystic, like so many other towns in the Black Hills, had been born on the promise of gold. Enough color was found in the hills immediately around Mystic to cause some of the more enterprising settlers to invest in real-estate, thus was born a town, complete with a leather-goods store, a laundry, a barbershop, a general-store, a livery, a hotel and three saloons. The barbershop was still going, but the leather-goods store and the laundry were already out of business, and the livery and general-store were just hanging on. The hotel was a little stronger, and the saloons were booming. In fact, ninety percent of the gold dug within a twenty-mile radius of Mystic passed through one of the saloons, so even with the other businesses having a rough time, the saloons were still profitable.

The saloons also served meals, and Sorghum and his companions were in the Goldenrod Saloon to take their supper. Sorghum had been here for a couple of days, waiting for the others, but Chewpack, Piedmont and Spaulding had arrived just this afternoon.

"I hear O'Toole's offered fifteen hundred dollars in gold to the man who kills Gunn," Sorghum said.

"I don't know why he's botherin'. Gunn's already dead, sure as hell," Chewpack said.

"What mades you think that?" Sorghum asked.

"Fergis liked to blowed him apart," Chewpack said. "Hell, you could've packed out what was left of that cabin in saddlebags."

"Yeah, but don't forget, that dynamite put a big hole in Fergis," Piedmont reminded him. "Then Gunn and that Indian gal with him rode off."

"Hell, that don't mean nothin'," Chewpack said. "I've seen rattlesnakes strike out and bite a man five minutes after they're dead. And they'll twitch 'til the sun goes down, you know that. My bet is he rode off somewhere and died."

"I don't know," Sorghum argued. "I'd say he's still alive."

"Then how come he ain't showed back in Deadwood? Answer me that," Chewpack wanted to know.

"Maybe he's decided to leave the country," Spaulding suggested.

"Yeah, that could be," Piedmont said. "We might not've killed him, but if he heard about the reward O'Toole's got out on him, then he probably wouldn't want to stick around."

"You fellas've never looked down the wrong end of a .45 at Gunn," Sorghum said. "I have. And believe me when I say he's not the kind you can just scare off, no matter how big a reward O'Toole has. He's killed how many now? He shot Meadows at the livery back in Deadwood, and he got the guards, Eddie and Mitch, there at the cabin. Then Fergis was killed when he blew up the cabin. And you said he got three more while you had the cabin under siege."

"We don't know that he got them," Chewpack said. "All we know is that someone from inside the cabin got them. The two women was shootin' too, don't forget."

"They was all three hit in the head," Spaulding said. "That wasn't no woman shootin', that was Gunn."

"That's eight," Sorghum said. He put his hand over the wound in his shoulder. "And he's taken me 'n Spence out of it. That makes ten. There's only ten left now, and that's includin' O'Toole. For a fella that's already taken out ten, I don't see him runnin' off because there are ten left."

"He would if it was the best ten," Chewpack said.

"Yeah," Spaulding added laughing. "He would if we were the best ten."

The waitress brought the men's supper then, and set the plates before the men. Chewpack picked up a pork chop and began eating it, pulling a piece of meat away from the bone with his mouth.

"I tell you," he said. "I been starvin' to death ever' since we run across that wagon. That sort'a thing always has made me hungry." A piece of fat fell off the pork chop and hung up in Chewpack's beard, but he didn't seem to notice.

"Watch your mouth," Spaulding said quickly, looking around the saloon. "You want ever'one in here to know what we done?"

Chewpack looked around the saloon. Chewpack and his friends were at a table way in the back. There were at least a dozen men standing at the bar, and about four tables full of drinkers or card players. The piano was banging away loudly, bottles and glasses were clinking, and everyone was talking so loud that there was almost a constant roar, like the rush of a wild river.

"Who the hell's going to hear us," Chewpack asked. "It's so loud in here I could probably fire my gun and no one would notice. Besides, no one is paying any attention to us."

"I want to keep it that way," Spaulding said.

"You say there was a little girl on that wagon?" Sorghum asked.

"Yeah," Chewpack said. "Prob'ly thirteen or fourteen. Somethin' like that."

"I'm . . . I'm glad I wasn't with you."

"Why? You got a thing for little girls?" Chewpack asked. He laughed. "If we'd'a knowed that, maybe we would'a brought her back to you so you could have a little fun beforehand."

"Alan, don't talk like that," Piedmont said.

"Oh, I see," Chewpack said. "It's all right to do it, just don't talk about it after you do it, right?"

"We . . . we didn't know there was a little girl on the wagon," Piedmont said.

"You didn't know there wasn't," Sorghum said.

"So what?" Chewpack said. He broke open the bone and began sucking on the marrow. "What about them Indian women and kids? That didn't slow anybody down none."

"They was Indians," Piedmont said. "The ones on

the wagon were white. They were our kind."

"Yeah, well they're both my kind," Chewpack said. "My maw was Indian. So white or Indian, it don't make no difference to me. You gonna suck on that bone?"

"What? No," Piedmont said.

Chewpack reached for it and took it off Piedmont's plate. "This here's the best part," he said as he snapped the bone in half.

The town of Mystic was laid out along a north-south axis. At the north end of town an enthusiastic group of town boosters, had erected a sign.

WELCOME TO MYSTIC

a little town with big ideas

WATCH US GROW!

population . . . 650

Gunn reached down and patted Esquire on the neck.

"Well, what do you say, fella? It'll be dark soon, would you like a warm stall tonight? Maybe some oats?"

Esquire blew, and Gunn chuckled softly.

"Thought you might," he said. He guided Esquire on into the town.

There was only one street in the town, a long dark corridor which stretched down between the false-fronted buildings.

The first building to the left was the leather-goods store. It was closed, and boards criss-crossed over the doors and windows, indicated that the closing was of a permanent nature. Next was a claims office, then a general store, both closed but, from appearances, closed only for the night. Beyond the general store was the office of the city marshal. It too, was closed.

On the right hand side, across the street, was a barber-shop, a couple of houses, then a livery stable. Esquire headed for the livery stable without having to be told. Gunn swung down from his horse and looked around. Ordinarily he would be met by the liveryman by now. No one showed up.

"Hello, the stable!" he called. He banged on the door, and called again. There was no answer. Finally, he pushed on the barn door, and it swung open, slowly, creaking as it did so.

"Hello," Gunn called again. "Anyone in here?"

Though the sun had not completely set, it was so low in the western sky that it was quite dark inside. Gunn saw a lantern hanging from the wall, and a little box of lucifers beside it. He struck a match and held the flame to the lantern mantle until it caught. He turned the key, and a soft glow of golden light bathed the inside of the barn. He re-hung the lantern on the hook where he had discovered it.

"Well, Esquire, looks like I get to tend to you myself," he said. Esquire whickered and nodded his head. Gunn chuckled and patted him on the face. "Yeah, you like it better when I take care of you, don't you?"

Gunn was cold, tired, hungry and thirsty. But he

had been a religious adherent to one rule for as long as he could remember. He always took care of his horse first.

Gunn took the saddle from Esquire's back and set it on the top bar of the first empty stall. He guided Esquire into the stall, then removed his bridle. A water trough ran across the end of the stall, and Esquire walked over and began drinking. Gunn found some oats and put them in the feeding trough, then rubbed his horse down.

When Gunn was finished, he closed the stall gate. He had still seen no one, but that wasn't important now. Esquire was taken care of. It was time for him to see to his own needs, and those needs started with a drink.

Some lights winked from the few private houses which were in town, but the most light came from the three saloons. They splashed big, golden squares of light out into the street, and even through doors closed against the winter chill, he could hear the sounds of people gathering together for communion with their own kind out here in the vast open spaces of the west. The first saloon he came to was the Goldenrod. A sign out front promised, "Whiskey, Beer, Eats". This was as good a place as any.

Gunn stepped through the door of the saloon, then moved out of the door so that his back was to the wall. It was a habit of his, developed specifically to lessen the chance of anyone shooting him in the back, but done now as such a matter of routine that he didn't even realize he was doing it. Another routine of Gunn's was to make a very careful check of everyone in the saloon before he moved in. If there were any enemies in the room, he wanted to know about them before he came any farther. He saw no one he knew, nor did he see anyone who looked as if they might represent danger to him. There were three, rough-looking men sitting around a table in the back of the room. From the settings on the table however, he knew that there had been a fourth, and he wondered where the fourth man might be. One of the three men, the one gnawing on the meat-bones, glanced toward Gunn. Gunn didn't know him, nor did he see any look of recognition on the part of the bone-sucker. As far as he could tell, there didn't seem to be any threat.

Gunn moved to a small table near the wall, and sat there, waiting for someone to come to him. The bartender sighed, then left the bar and walked over to the table.

"Most folks by themselves come to the bar," he said.

"I like it here."

"So I see. All right, what can I do for you, Mister? What do you want?"

"Whiskey, if it's anything but Canadian Prime."

"I can accommodate you."

"The sign says eats," Gunn said.

"Pork chops and fried potatoes tonight. Take it or leave it, that's what we have."

"Whiskey now, a glass of beer with my supper," Gunn said.

The bartender left. A moment later he brought a bottle and a glass and left them on the table.

"Mary Lou or Emma Jean will see to your supper," he said. "If both of 'em's been took upstairs, I'll have the cook bring it out."

Gunn nodded toward the men at the back table. "You know them?" he asked.

"They've been in here before," the bartender answered. "But I don't know them. I don't know you either, and I don't want to know. It ain't my job to know people, just to sell 'em what they want to drink."

Gunn poured himself a glass of whiskey as the bartender returned to his bar, and he studied the three men over the rim of his glass. There was something about them . . . something he couldn't quite put his finger on.

"You sure you don't want to spend the night?" Emma Jean asked. "I can give you a good price on spending the night. Nearly as good as you'll get across the street at the hotel, only here, you'll have company."

"I don't need company," Sorghum said. He pulled on his boot, then winced with pain as the action caused his shoulder wound to hurt.

"You all right, honey?" Emma Jean asked. Emma Jean was one of the two waitresses working at the saloon, and the one who had given Sorghum and the others their supper. Sorghum had been in town for three days, and this was the third time in as many days, that he had taken Emma Jean upstairs. It was the fact that he kept coming back to her that prompted Emma Jean to suggest that he might want to spend the night with her, rather than rejoining his friends.

"Yeah," Sorghum answered. "I'm fine. Just a little sore, that's all." Sorghum stood up.

The woman, realizing then that she would be unable to talk him into staying all night, sighed and reached for her dress. She had wanted him to stay with her because she was afraid that if she went back downstairs now, one of his friends would want her. She would prefer to have nothing to do with them, if possible.

Sorghum stepped out into the hallway, and started for the stairs. Just as he came out on the landing, however, he happened to look down onto the room below. That was when he saw Gunn, calmly eating his supper.

"Gunn!" he said.

"Why, you've got your gun on, honey," Emma Jean said from behind him.

Sorghum stepped back into the shadows, and when Emma Jean started to go around him, he reached for her. "No!" he hissed.

"What is it, honey? What's wrong?"

"Don't go down there, yet."

"Honey, I've got to go down there. Else if I stay up here, you'll have to pay for another visit. Or, for all night."

"All right, I'll stay all night," Sorghum said.

"Well, that's more like it," Emma Jean said, smiling broadly.

Sorghum peeked around the corner, surveying the scene below. He could see Gunn, and he could see Chewpack, Piedmont and Spaulding. Surely they could see each other, why were they all just sitting so quietly?

Suddenly Sorghum realized why Gunn and the others were sitting calmly. Their only previous encounter had been at the siege at the cabin. There, they had been separated by a distance of several yards, plus they had the cover of the trees, rocks, and the cabin wall itself. In addition to all that, there was also the gunsmoke, and the confusion of the moment. Chewpack, Piedmont and Spaulding hadn't recognized Gunn, and he didn't recognize them.

Sorghum wondered for a moment what he should do. If he started down the stairs, Gunn would recognize him right away. But he needed to let Chewpack and the others know.

"Emma Jean, I want you to go downstairs and tell Chewpack to come up here."

"What?" Emma Jean asked. She blanched, and shook her head. "Look here, honey, I don't know what you got in mind, but I'll only be with one at a time. And if you're payin' me for all night, there can't nobody else get a free ride on your ticket."

"It ain't that," Sorghum said. "It's . . ." Sorghum stopped in mid-sentence. Wait a minute! Why should he share that fifteen hundred dollars with the others? "Never mind," he said. "You got another way outta this place?"

"Are you leavin', honey?"

Sorghum took out ten dollars and gave it to Emma Jean. "Yeah, but don't worry, I'll be back. You just keep the bed warm for me. Now, is there a back way out?"

"Through the kitchen is all. They's a back set of stairs leads down into the kitchen, then the kitchen door leads outside."

Sorghum pulled his pistol and checked his loads, then chuckled. This is the way Meadows should've done it in the first place. He had no business trying to brace Gunn.

With his gun still in his hand, Sorghum walked down the back stairs and came out into the kitchen. The kitchen was hot with the cooking fires, and smelled of grease and condiments. An old woman stood over one of the stoves, frying pork chops. She was smoking a pipe, and she looked around when she heard Sorghum coming down the stairs. Her eyes grew wide with fright when she saw Sorghum carrying his gun.

"What do you want?" she asked, frightened by the sudden appearance of an armed man in her kitchen.

"Don't worry about it, old woman," Sorghum said. "All I'm lookin' for is a way outta here. Where's the back door?"

The old woman pulled her pipe from her mouth, and using the stem as a pointer, indicated the back door.

Sorghum chuckled to himself as he walked out the door. "Fifteen hundred dollars," he said. "I'm goin' to take it 'n go to California."

It was already dark outside, and with the dark came a drop in temperature. Sorghum hurried along behind the buildings until he found a narrow walk space where he could pass between them. He moved between the buildings to the street, then crossed the street to the boarded up leather-goods shop. He stepped back into the shadow and looked at the front door of the Goldenrod Saloon. He would have a perfect shot at Gunn the moment Gunn came out.

* * *

Gunn finished his supper then looked over toward a near-by table where four men were playing cards. For a moment he considered sitting in on it. It had been a while since he'd had the relaxation of a good game of poker. But it seemed even longer since he had enjoyed a real bed, and the idea of a bed seemed more inviting than a hand of poker, even if he held a full house. He sighed. Maybe tomorrow. And maybe tomorrow he would be able to get a lead on O'Toole.

The woman who served him came to pick up his empty plate. She smiled at him.

"Anything else you be wantin', mister?"

"I don't think so," Gunn said.

The woman leaned over to show Gunn a generous amount of cleavage.

"Are you sure?" she asked, throatily. "I can show you a good time. A real good time."

Gunn smiled at her. "I'm sure you could at that," he said. "But I think I'll pass this time."

"You worried about the cost?" the woman asked. "Because if you are, you can stop worryin'. For you, it won't cost a thing."

"Oh? You can't make a living that way, can you?"

"Maybe not. But a girl that's on the line like me, ever' now'n again I got to have someone that I really want to have, you know what I mean? Otherwise the whole thing'll get to be so borin' that I just lose interest. The worse thing can happen is for a whore to lose interest in men."

"I can see where that might be a problem," Gunn said. "I'm sorry I can't help you. Maybe some other

111

time." Gunn got up to leave, and the woman reached down and patted him on the crotch.

"It would'a been good, honey," she said. "Real good."

Sorghum was so cold that his fingers were beginning to go stiff on him. The cold was also causing his wound to hurt, and the more it hurt, the more satisfaction he took out of waiting for Gunn. Sure, he wanted the money. But all he had to do was think of the bullet hole in his shoulder, and he was ready to kill Gunn for free.

Suddenly, he heard a footfall on the boardwalk outside the saloon.

A flush of heat shot through Sorghum as he stepped out of the shadows. He had the drop on the tall man. He wanted to see the look in Gunn's eyes when he went down.

"Gunn, you sonafabitch, I'm callin' you out," he shouted. But he stayed in the shadows between the two buildings.

A passerby heard the voice, ducked out of the way.

"I don't see anybody," said Gunn quietly. But his voice carried.

"Draw, you bastard," snarled Sorghum.

Gunn held his ground, but he stepped out of the light that spilled through the half-open door of the saloon. He crouched slightly, his figure etched in shadow, his right hand hovering over the butt of his pistol.

Sorghum stretched his neck to see. He made out the bare outline of Gunn, standing to one side of the aloon door.

"I'm waiting," said Gunn patiently.

Sorghum drew in a breath. It was now or never. He still had the advantage. Gunn had not drawn his pistol. Sorghum slipped his own pistol from its holster, stepped around the corner of the building. He brought his pistol up fast, aimed at the shadowy man on the boardwalk. He cocked on the rise, tried to steady down on his target. The cold came back then, shivering through him like a north wind. His hand shook slightly. He fired twice as he came around the corner, blindly, counting on confusion to give him the edge.

Explosions lit the night and the bullets went wild, smashing out windows, caroming off a roof.

Sorghum took full aim, then, knowing he was exposed.

Gunn saw the movement, saw the dark shine of the pistol barrel as it caught the light, like a fish jumping from night waters. His hand flashed, faster than the eye could follow, and the leather of his holster whispered against the steel.

Gunn's thumb cocked the hammer back as the gun cleared leather and he deepened his crouch. A flare of bright orange flashed from across the street, but he was already squeezing the trigger of his Colt. The pistol bucked in his hand, and white smoke billowed out behind the fireflash of black powder. Just over his head he heard the brief whine-buzz of the assassin's bullet and the thunk of lead into wood. Sorghum cracked off another shot, but it spat into the dirt a good six feet in front of Gunn.

"You made a mistake, mister," Gunn muttered as

113

the man across the street crumpled. He knew from the sound that his bullet had gone home, somewhere in the chest, high, near the heart. He heard the ugly sound of a man's breath leaving him suddenly.

Sorghum fell with a thud, as people rushed out of the saloon, and a man bulled his way down the street toward him.

Gunn waited. Smoke curled upward from the muzzle of his pistol. He cocked the single action, looking around.

The man in a hurry stepped up on the boardwalk.

"I'm the marshal of Mystic," he said to Gunn.

"It was self-defense, marshal, I seen it all," someone said. He was the one who had ducked out of danger when he first heard Sorghum call Gunn out. "This here tall fella just come out of the saloon when the dead man here commenced firin' at him from behind this buildin'. The truth is, I wouldn't have given a Chinaman's chance in hell for the tall fella here, but he just stood his ground calm as you please, 'n after three or four shots he fired back one time and that's all there was to it."

"Is that the way it happened?" the marshal asked.

"He only fired two fair shots at me," Gunn replied.

"Did you know this fella?"

"Not really," Gunn said.

"What do you mean, not really? You either know'd him or you didn't"

"I don't know his name, but this is the second time he's tried to kill me," Gunn said. "If you'll check his shoulder, you'll see there's a bullet wound not more'n a week old. I put it there."

"He tried before, huh? Seems to me like he was a

114

ow learner. You got any idea why he tried to kill
ou?"

"Revenge, I guess."

"Seems as good a motive as any." The marshal
nelt down and started looking through the dead
nan's pockets.

"Maybe there'll be somethin' here that'll tell us who
e is." The marshal looked up at the crowd. "Any-
ody know him?"

"I . . ." Spaulding started, but Chewpack poked
im hard with his elbow.

"You what?" The marshal asked.

"I seen him in the Goldenrod while ago, is all,"
paulding said.

Gunn noticed that Spaulding was one of the men
e had seen at the table in the back of the room.

"He's got twelve dollars on him," the marshal said.
he marshal looked at a tall, thin man. "Will you
ury him for that, Estes?"

"Won't be a very grand buryin'," Estes said.

"Just so's you get 'im in the ground," the marshal
aid.

"Reckon I can do that," Estes agreed.

"All right, he's yours," the marshal said. "Rest of
ou folks, get on about your business."

"Ain't you gonna ask this here fella his name?"
Chewpack suddenly asked the marshal.

"His name? What do I need to know that for? We
lready know it was self-defense."

"Don't make no never mind, you need to know the
ella's name," Chewpack insisted.

"William Gunnison," Gunn said.

"Huh?" Chewpack asked, confused by the answer.

115

"Most folks call me Gunn," Gunn said, smiling at Chewpack. Now he knew what had disturbed him about Chewpack and the others. They were O'Toole's men.

That was good to know.

Chapter Nine

"It's room two-oh-seven, Mr. Gunn," the hotel clerk said. "Upstairs, all the way to the back, first door on the left."

"Thanks." Gunn replied, signing the registration book.

"I do hope you enjoy your stay with us," the clerk went on. "We're quite proud of our little town here."

Gunn draped his saddlebags over his shoulder, then climbed the stairs to the second floor, where he came upon a long hallway. The hall carpet was maroon with a floral-design, the wallpaper light brown with dark brown stripes. Kerosene lanterns were mounted on the wall between every door and all were burning brightly so that the hall was well lighted. There were three rooms on each side of the hall, then, at the end of the hall there was a "T". Room 207 was the first door to the left of the "T". At the end of the "T" there was a window which opened outside. Gunn extinguished the lantern nearest the window so he could stand in the shadow, then he stood to one side and peeked through the curtain. Even though it was dark outside, there was enough light from the moon, and from the lights of the saloons, to allow him to see three men standing in the middle of the street. He could even tell that they were the same three he had seen in the back of the saloon. They were talking animatedly. One of them pointed to the leather-goods shop where Gunn had shot his assailant, and another pointed toward the hotel. Gunn knew they were talking about him, and he surmised that whatever they were saying bode him no good.

Gunn returned to his room, unlocked the door, and went inside. It was a typical hotel room, consisting of a bed, a washstand, and a lamptable. Gunn opened the window.

"Why didn't he come tell us, if he seen Gunn?" Piedmont wanted to know.

" 'Cause he wanted the reward his ownself, that's why," Chewpack replied.

"Yeah. Well, that's what you get for bein' greedy," Piedmont said.

"You don't have to worry none 'bout me bein' greedy," Spaulding assured the others. "I wouldn't try'n take Gunn myself for five thousand dollars, let alone fifteen hundred."

"No, me neither," Piedmont agreed.

"No, but if the three of us took him, it would be worth five hundred each for us," Chewpack suggested.

"What good is five hundred dollars to a dead man?" Spaulding asked. "No, sir, you can just count me out. Look what happened to Meadows, Spense

118

nd Sorghum when they tried him. They was three of hem and that didn't mean nothin'."

"Meadows tried to brace him," Chewpack ex-lained. "He was a fool, and he thought he could andle anybody. Well, I ain't no fool, and I don't aim o brace Gunn. I got me a better idea . . . an idea that an't miss."

"Yeah?" Spaulding said. "I bet Sorghum thought e had a pretty good idea too. Hide behind a building n the dark and shoot him when he walks by. What an be safer than that? Only it wasn't safe, was it? orghum got hisself killed."

Chewpack smiled. "Uh, huh. But instead of just ne person, what if three people drygulched Gunn? And what if they done it while Gunn was asleep?"

"Asleep?"

"Yeah," Chewpack replied. He smiled broadly, as if n self-congratulations over his brilliant idea.

"How you gonna do that?"

"It's easy. We just find out what room Gunn's taying in over at the hotel. Then we just go over there nd blast away while he's asleep."

"Hey, yeah, not bad," Piedmont said, understand-ng then what Chewpack was saying. "That sounds ike a good idea. What do you think, Earl? Is that a ;ood idea or not?"

"I'm not so sure," Spaulding hesitated.

"Well, to hell with you if you don't want to do it," Chewpack said. "We'll just do it without you. That'll e more money for us."

"Hold on, hold on, I didn't say I didn't want to do t," Spaulding responded quickly. "I just said I didn't now if it was a good idea or not."

119

"Well, are you, or ain't you?"

"All right, I'll do it," Spaulding agreed. "But let's not take no chances, all right? I mean once we start shootin', let's empty our guns into the son of a bitch. We can't give him no chance to shoot back. If we do, we're dead men, sure'n hell."

"He just went up there," Piedmont said. "You think he's asleep yet?"

"I doubt it. But come on, let's go back to the saloon and have a few more drinks. That'll give him plenty of time to get to sleep," Chewpack suggested.

Gunn pulled the cord from the carpet. He spliced it in three places, so that now he had a string that was sixty feet long. Of course the hotel wouldn't appreciate what Gunn was doing to their rug, but that couldn't be helped. If he was going to get any sleep tonight, he was going to have to have some way of being warned if anyone tried to sneak up on him. Once Gunn had the string prepared, he went to work. He tied one end of his line to a nail about four inches above the floor, stretched the cord across the hallway, then looped it around another nail at about the same height on the opposite side. After that he turned out all the lanterns on his end of the hallway, so that the "T" would be very dark. He stepped back to look at it, and saw that it was completely invisible to anyone who might be walking down the corridor. Gunn took the loose end of the string, passed it under his door and into his room. Once inside his room, he tied the end of the cord to his big toe, then went to bed.

* * *

It was nearly midnight when Chewpack, Piedmont and Spaulding left the saloon. They stood just outside the saloon door and buttoned their coats up against the cold. A burst of laughter floated across the street from one of the other saloons.

"Sounds like they're havin' a good time over there," Piedmont said. "Maybe we should'a waited there."

"When we get the money, we can wait in all three of them," Chewpack suggested.

"Abel, you think he's asleep now?" Spaulding asked.

"Yeah, it's nearly midnight, ain't it? That's plenty late enough for him to be asleep."

"I hope you're right. I sure don't want to come up on him, him bein' awake."

"Look, he's been out in the hills for a long time. This is the first warm bed he's had in a week. What do you think?"

"Maybe he got hisself a woman for the night," Piedmont suggested.

Chewpack laughed. "If he did, he's finished with her now, that's for sure. Anyhow, that's all the better. You know what it's like when you're with a woman 'n you're tired 'n cold. Hell, when you finished, you can't wait to go to sleep. And then you sleep like a baby. Gunn's asleep, all right, and he ain't gonna wake up. Fact is, when we get through with him, he ain't never gonna wake up."

They started walking toward the hotel then, with their boots clumping loudly on the boardwalk, and the vapor of their breath forming a little cloud over their heads.

"What if the woman's still with him?"

"She probably ain't."

"But what if she is?"

"If she is, she is."

"But if we just start shootin', she'll be in the way."

"What the hell difference does that make? You've killed women before."

"Yeah, but, never in town."

Chewpack laughed again. "The ones you kill outta town are just as dead as the ones you kill in town."

They stepped into the hotel. The lobby was warmed by a fire in the lobby stove, and it was lighted by overhead lamps. It was dark in the area behind the registration desk, and when they looked over there, they could see why. The clerk had extinguished the lantern and he had his chair tipped back against the wall, his arms folded across his chest, his eyes closed, and his mouth open. His snoring was quite audible.

"The clerk's asleep," Spaulding said.

"Just as well," Chewpack said. "We don't need ever'one knowin' our business. Besides, I want to take a look at the registration book. Sometimes they get a little touchy about that."

"What do you need to look at the book for?"

"To see which room he's in," Chewpack said impatiently. "Wait here. If all of us go over there, we might wake him up."

Chewpack walked quietly over to the desk, turned the book around and looked at it. About three fourths of the way down the page he saw what he was looking for. "Gunn, Rm 207."

"Did you find out?" Piedmont whispered, when

Chewpack rejoined them.

"Yeah," Chewpack answered. "I know where he is. Come on, let's go."

The three men slipped their pistols out of their holsters, then walked slowly up the carpeted stairway. Once they reached the top of the stairs, they started for the back. From behind the closed doors which lined the wall on either side of them, they could hear the snores and deep breathing of the hotel guests. All were sleeping peacefully, unaware of the life and death game about to take place in their midst.

"All these here lanterns is out," Piedmont said. "I'll light one of 'em, if it ain't out of coal oil."

"Don't bother," Chewpack said.

"But it's dark back here . . . so dark I can't even read the room numbers."

"We want it like that," Chewpack insisted. "When we open the door, we don't want no light shining behind us."

"The only thing is, how can we be sure we got the right door?"

"If you're that worried about it, when we get there, I'll strike a match, just to be sure. That way we'll . . . uhn! Watch where the hell you're goin', Earl!"

"It ain't my fault," Spaulding complained. "This here carpet's comin apart. I tripped over a loose string."

When Spaulding hit the string, Gunn felt a sudden pull on his toe and it woke him up instantly. He sat up in bed and took the cord off his toe, then moved quickly to the window. Quietly, he slid the window up, then stepped out onto the ledge. There was no snow or ice on the ledge, but it was cold to his bare feet, nevertheless.

Gunn started working his way toward the next window. From the building next door, he could hear the squeaking of a sign being blown in the wind. From farther away, out on the plains, he could hear the lonesome call of a coyote. The tinkling notes of a piano played by a weary musician who was still having to entertain the saloon crowd, reached his ears. Then, a moment later, he was outside the next window. Slowly, he began to slide it open.

Caitlin had no idea how long she had been asleep when something awakened her. She sat up abruptly, senses attuned to whatever had disturbed her sleep. Then she heard it, the faint scraping sound of her window. Curious now, she struck a match to light the lamp. The wick flamed up, illuminating the room, and she swung her feet over the edge of the bed and walked toward the window, dressed only in a white silk nightgown.

It was typical of Caitlin that she would go toward the sound, rather than away from it, for, though only twenty-one, Caitlin was already a young woman of immense courage and unbridled curiosity. Thus it was that the principal question in her mind was more of who was at her window than why.

The window came open, and a pair of long legs slid through, followed by a torso, and then by a head.

"Who the hell are you, and what do you want?" Caitlin asked the tall man who had just let himself, uninvited, into her room.

Gunn looked at the woman who had just challenged him. She was a beauty, with flaming red hair, green eyes, a slender waist, and well formed breasts, the nipples of which were easily visible in relief, under her silk nightgown.

"Good evening," Gunn whispered. "My name is Gunn, and I just came in to get out of the cold."

"Well, as you can clearly see, this room is occupied," Caitlin said. "So I'll thank you to just get back out."

"Yes," Gunn said. "And so I shall."

"Now," Caitlin said.

"Yes, right away," Gunn replied, almost as if distracted by something else. "If you will excuse me then, I'll just be out of your way." Gunn pulled his pistol and held it down by his side.

"What is that?" Caitlin asked, looking at the pistol. "What do you need with a gun?"

"Shhh," Gunn whispered, holding his finger over his lips. Gunn walked quietly over to the door, opened it just a crack, then looked out into the corridor.

"Just as I thought," he said. "They're there."

"Who's there?"

Gunn held his finger to his lips again.

Caitlin couldn't believe what was happening to her. Two minutes ago she was sound asleep, now she was standing in her room watching someone with a gun, a perfect stranger who had just barged in on her. It was a frightening experience. And yet, despite the fright, Caitlin was vaguely aware of another sensation which she didn't fully understand. She was experiencing a degree of excitement and pleasure. She couldn't explain it, but neither could she deny it. The idea of a man as handsome as this one, coming into her room at night, catching her practically nude, was terribly exciting. Add to that the degree of danger which was inherent in the situation, and Caitlin could feel her blood running warm.

Suddenly Caitlin heard a crashing sound as the door in the room next door was smashed in. "Kill the bastard!" someone shouted. Immediately after the shout, she heard the explosion of gunshots, not just one or two, but many, as if war had been declared, and the opening battle was being fought here in this very hotel.

To Caitlin's surprise, the man who had come into her room suddenly stepped out into the hall.

"I'm over here!" Gunn spoke.

"What the hell?" Chewpack shouted in surprise.

"Shoot him! Kill him! Don't let him get away!" one of the three men yelled, and all three men turned their pistols toward Gunn and began blazing away.

Though dark from the lack of lanterns, the hall was now brightly lighted by a series of brilliant orange flashes as four guns roared. The noise was deafening, and the smoke rolled in such a big cloud that it looked as if the hotel were on fire. When the smoke was finally gone, and the last gunshot a distant echo, three men lay dead or dying while Gunn stood without a scratch.

Caitlin had not screamed. In fact, she had made no sound whatever while the drama was being played out before her. Now she stepped to the door of her room and looked out into the hall.

"Are you all right?" she asked Gunn. For some reason, it was important to her that he be unhurt.

"Yeah, I'm fine," Gunn said.

"What is it? What's going on out here?" a man asked, stepping out of one of the rooms. He had on a robe, house-slippers, and a night-cap. "Can't a body get any sleep around here?"

"Sounds to me like all hell broke loose," someone said. "Sounded like the war, all over again."

"Is it over?"

Those who had been sleeping so peacefully but a few seconds earlier were now moving cautiously from their rooms, edging slowing down the hallway, looking on with fearful eyes at the carnage Gunn had wrought. The hall was heavy with the smell of cordite.

Spaulding and Piedmont were both dead, Chewpack was dying. Gunn knelt beside him.

"Mister," Chewpack said. A coughing spasm seized him, and he hacked for a moment before he spoke again. "You're one hard man to kill, you know that?"

"I try to be," Gunn said.

Chewpack laughed. "My pa said I'd be hung," he said. "And look at me. Goin' out in a blaze of glory. My pa always was a dumb son of a bitch." Chewpack coughed again. "That's why I shot him." He tried once more to cough the blood out of his lungs, but this time he couldn't do it. After a few wheezing efforts, he died. Gunn punched the expended shell casings from his pistol, then put fresh loads in. He had fired only three times, whereas the three dead men had nearly emptied their guns.

"My," the clerk said, looking at the dead men, the smashed door, and the bullet holes in the walls and in Gunn's bed. "Oh, my."

"I'll be needing another room," Gunn said matter-of-factly.

"What?"

"A room," Gunn said. "I'll be needing another. The bed is all shot up in this one. The ticking is falling out."

"Uh, yes," the clerk said. "Yes, of course. I'll get you another room." He looked back at the bodies and shook his head as if in shock. "My," he said again. "My oh my."

"Let me through, let me through," a new, authoritative voice said, and the people, all of whom were wearing robes and dressing gowns, opened up to let the new arrival through. It was the marshal.

"Hello, marshal," Gunn greeted.

The marshal saw Gunn, then he looked at the three bodies. "You do this?"

"I guess I did," Gunn answered.

"Mister, what's the matter with you? You on a one man campaign to kill ever'one in Mystic?"

"I could turn that around," Gunn said, "and ask you if Mystic is out to get me. As you can see by my room, they came up here and started firin'."

"Marshal, I don't know if it means anything," one of the guests volunteered. "But I seen these here three men with that man that this fella killed earlier tonight. They was all together over in the Golden-rod."

"You have any idea why they were trying to kill

you?"

"No," Gunn said.

The marshal sighed. "Well, as far as you know, is anyone else in town trying to kill you? I mean if they are I'd better get the undertaker outta bed 'n tell him he's gonna be workin' all night."

"I don't know if anyone else is trying to kill me," Gunn said. "I didn't know these men were. Look, marshal, all I want to do is get a good night's sleep, then leave your fair town tomorrow."

"Yeah, leave it tomorrow," the marshal said. "That's a good idea."

"I can let you have room two-eleven," the clerk volunteered. "It's empty."

"Thanks," Gunn said.

"I'll get the key." The clerk left.

"All right, folks, it's all over now," the marshal said. "Suppose you people just go on back to bed and forget about it. It's all over."

The spectators began returning to their rooms then, so that, a moment later, only Gunn, the marshal, and Caitlin were still there.

"I'll get these bodies took care of. But that's twice I've been called out of a warm house to clean up your mess. Don't do it again."

Gunn watched the marshal leave, then he was aware that the woman was still watching him. He looked around at her.

"Miss, I'm much obliged to you for letting me use your room," he said.

Caitlin smiled at him. "You've no idea what sort of thoughts went through my mind when you came through my window," she said.

129

"What sort of thoughts?"

"I thought maybe you were coming to rape me."

"No, ma'am. I would never rape a woman," Gunn said.

Caitlin smiled again. "No, I don't suppose you would. The truth is, I don't think you would have to. I think you could probably get a woman to do just about anything you asked. I know I would."

The woman's frankness embarrassed Gunn and he cleared his throat and looked away.

"I'll keep that in mind if I ever need a favor," Gunn mumbled.

Chapter Ten

Taylor tied his horse to the lowest branch of a pine tree, then moved down the side of the hill through the dark shadows, toward the camp. The coals from the campfire glowed cherry red in the darkness, and in the small bubble of light the campfire put out, Taylor could see three men. He knew they were prospectors, because he had been following their trail all day. He saw one of the men throw wood onto the fire, then stir it into crackling flames which danced merrily against the bottom of a suspended coffee pot.

"What are you gonna do with your money?" the man who had just added wood to the fire asked. He was tall and thin.

"I'm goin' to Denver. I'm gonna get me a woman, two bottles of whiskey and a big steak dinner," one of the others answered. He was a little shorter than the first, but was most distinguishable by the fact that he was the only one of the three with a beard.

"I'm gonna get two women, and one bottle of whiskey," the tall man said, then he laughed and added; "And I'm gonna forget about the steak dinner."

"What about you, Lee? What you gonna do?"

"I've got plans," the one called Lee replied.

"We know what he's gonna do," the tall man said "He's gonna do the right thing."

"That's what we should do too," the bearded on replied."

"Yeah, I know. The smart thing to do would be t save the money, or put it into some business," the tal man agreed.

"That's the smart thing to do."

"I've changed my mind. I'm not gonna get tw women," the tall man said.

"You're not?" the bearded one asked.

"No, I'm gonna get *three* women."

All three prospectors laughed again.

Taylor smiled as he heard the prospectors bante back and forth. O'Toole's men had cut the prospec tor's trail early this morning. Most prospector trail meandered around quite a bit, searching here, there everywhere, trying to find the elusive stuff of thei dreams. This trail, however, was unwandering an definite. O'Toole reasoned that it was because th men had already found something, and were on thei way out of the hills. To test his theory, he sent Taylo to find them.

Taylor remained in the shadows while he checke the prospectors out. He saw that none of the thre were wearing gunbelts, nor did any of them have thei weapons in easy reach. That was good, otherwise h could easily get shot if he suddenly walked in o them. The way it was right now, the advantage wa with him. He took a deep breath, then stood up and walked boldly, almost brazenly into their camp.

"What the hell?" the tall man said, seeing Taylor suddenly materialize out of the night. "Who are you, mister? And what the hell are you doing here?"

"I seen your fire, 'n I smelt your coffee, 'n I was hopin' you'd be gentlemen enough to share some of your bounty."

"Who are you?" Lee asked.

"A poor prospector," Taylor answered, "like yourselves, only, my partners were killed, and my horse and all my possibles were stole by a wanderin' bunch of murderin' redskins. I . . . I ain't et nothin' in two days, 'n I was hopin' you could spare a mite of food."

Lee Butler had felt the hackles rise on the back of his neck at the moment of the unexpected intrusion. He looked over toward their sleeping bags and saw the six bags of gold dust. He knew that some men would kill for a pinch from any one of these bags . . . for six full bags even the most cautious might be moved to bold recklessness. Lee wished they had taken the precaution of at least putting the bags out of sight, though they had seen no one for weeks, and had no expectations of company tonight.

Lee's instinct was to turn the man away, send him off into the night. But, if the man had really been without food for two days, that would be an unkind act. On the other hand, if they gave him food, and acted as if they had nothing to hide, perhaps the man would have cause to suspect nothing, and go on along his way, giving them no trouble.

"I don't know . . ." the bearded one started to say, but Lee interrupted him.

"We've got a few beans left over," he said. "Some

133

fresh coffee. We'd be pleased to help a fellow prospector down on his luck."

"Bless you, sir," Taylor said. "Bless you." He hurried over to the fire and picked up a cup and held it, while coffee was poured. Lee dished up a pan of beans and handed it to him, and Taylor ate them, wolfing them down as if he really hadn't eaten in two days. He hadn't eaten supper, and that made it easier for him to carry out the illusion of real hunger.

"You say you were jumped by Indians?"

"Yes."

" 'S' funny. The only ones we've seen have been friendly enough to us," Lee said. "We've traded tobacco and coffee for meat a couple of times."

"Yeah," the tall man said. "We ain't seen nothin' to fear from them."

"They can be like that," Taylor explained. "One minute just friendly as you please, 'n the next, wild as a beast. That's the way they was when they attacked that settler's wagon last week, killed him 'n his wife 'n daughter."

"That a fact? I haven't heard of that," Lee said.

"Oh, yeah, it's all over the hills," Taylor said. "Tell me, have you gentlemen had any luck?"

Taylor watched the expressions on the face of the three men as he asked the question. They all looked at each other, and it was as plain as the nose on their face that they were trying to hide their success. Finally, the one who had offered him food, spoke.

"Uh, no," Lee said. "Not so much as a speck of color."

"Well," Taylor said, standing up and putting down his now empty cup and pan. "Keep tryin'. You'll find somethin', I'm sure. I'm much obliged for the vittles. I'll be on my way now."

"Where you goin?"

"I'm walkin' back to the nearest settlement where I can buy another horse."

"You wanna stay the night?"

"No, thanks, I'd better be gettin' on."

"Good luck," Lee called, watching as the man disappeared into the dark.

"Why'd you ask him to stay?" the bearded one asked.

" 'Cause if he's plannin' anything, I'd rather have him where we can see him than out in the dark where we can't," Lee replied.

"Do you think he's gonna try somethin'?"

"Could be," Lee answered. "At any rate, just to be on the safe side, I think we should keep our guns with us for the rest of the night."

"You might be right," the tall man said. "We worked too damn hard for what we got to give it up to some dry-gulcher."

"I'll take the first watch," Lee offered. "I think one of us should stay awake all night."

"All right. I'll take second," the tall man volunteered.

"I guess that leaves me third," the bearded one said.

Lee watched as the others got into their bedrolls to go to sleep. He threw a chunk of wood on the fire then moved closer for its warmth, and wrapped his hands around his Winchester and waited. If anybody else came tonight, he was going to be prepared for them.

Lee was from Georgia. He had returned home

from the war to find his farm gone and his wife and kids living with her relatives. He tried a little share-cropping, but that didn't work out too well. Then, when it appeared that there was nothing left for him in Georgia, he came to South Dakota, intending to dig out just enough gold to enable him to buy a farm in Oregon.

For three years Lee had been searching. In all that time he found no canyon too treacherous to descend, no river too dangerous to cross, no mountain too difficult to climb. Occasionally he would find just enough color to provide him with an on-going grub-stake, but he never found enough to get out of it with a profit.

Then, four weeks ago, he and his two partners were searching along the Bear Butte River, scanning the river bed for bars of gravel where gold flakes often collected. When he found a likely looking bar, he dug up some sand and put it in his pan, swished water around it until all the light sand was washed out, then gasped. There, in the bottom of his pan, were a few tiny, but heavy yellow flakes of gold.

Lee let out a yell for his partners. They came over, saw what he had discovered, and fell immediately to working the same bar. Over the last four weeks the three men had panned more than $6,000 worth of dust. They had found nothing for the last three days however, and were now convinced that they had taken all the gold there was to take from that one location.

Lee was satisfied. His share was $2,200, a little more because he got the "finder's fee," and plenty enough for him to start a farm in Oregon. He was going to start for Oregon, first thing tomorrow, buy his farm, then send for his family.

O'Toole was eating a supper of whiskey and jerky when Taylor came riding back into camp. Taylor swung off his horse and approached O'Toole, who gave him a drink from his bottle.

"Did you find their camp?" O'Toole asked.

"I found them," Taylor said.

"And would they be havin' gold with them?" O'Toole offered a piece of jerky to Taylor, but Taylor declined with a shake of his head.

"I already ate," he said. "The prospectors fed me while I looked over their camp." Taylor laughed. "They say they ain't had no luck, but I heard 'em talkin' just before I walked in on 'em. They got gold, all right."

"Where are they?"

"They're camped where the Bear Butte and the Belle Fourche meet, just like you said they would be."

O'Toole chuckled. "Aye, and the soldier boys are up on the Sulphur, just like the schedule says. 'Tis a fine operation we've got going now, lad, what with us always knowin' just where to find the army, 'n takin' advantage of the fact."

"Yeah," Taylor said. "Now if we just knew where Gunn was."

"Aye, Gunn," O'Toole spat. " 'Tis the devil's own lieutenant, Gunn is. He shot down four good men in Mystic."

"We've got to do something about him," Taylor insisted.

"You let me worry about our friend Gunn,"

O'Toole said. He smiled. "For now, let's just think about the minin' camp ahead, and all that fine gold dust they'll be carryin'.

"Are we going to hit them tonight?"

"Tell me, Taylor, would they be suspectin' you?"

"I think so," Taylor said. "When I asked them if they had any luck, I could tell by the way they were lookin' at one another that they didn't trust me."

O'Toole smiled. "Ah, that's good, that's good. We'll wait 'n hit 'em in the mornin'."

"Why wait?"

"Don't you see, lad? With them suspectin' you, they'll like as not keep one awake all night long. And even the ones not awake will not be sleepin' all that good. They'll be tired in the mornin'. That'll be a fine time to hit them. That way, we'll only need three of us to hit the miners. At the same time we're about that business, Smitty, Hollifield and Morgan can hit the Indian camp we saw this afternoon. That'll keep things stirred up, good 'n proper."

"I gotta hand it to you, O'Toole. You're a genius."

"Aye," O'Toole agreed immodestly. "I am at that."

Gunn saw the Indian camp just after sundown. There were only about half a dozen tipis, but smoke was curling from the top of all of them, and he could smell the rich aroma of buffalo stew. In the remuda, he recognized the horse Smoke Eyes had been riding when last he saw her, so he took a chance that she would be here. If so, he was certain he would be warmly welcomed. If not, he might have a difficult time.

One of the tipi flaps opened, and he glimpsed the warm wink of a fire inside. A young woman stepped through the flap and he recognized Smoke Eyes. He smiled at her.

"Hello, Smoke Eyes," he said. He swung down from his horse.

"Hello, Gunn. Why have you come?"

"I saw the camp, I smelled the stew," Gunn said. "It made me hungry."

By now, a dozen others had come out of their tipis to see what was going on. There were three warriors among the dozen, and they were all carrying their rifles. Of course, as a rifle was the Indian's most valuable possession, Gunn knew that the fact the warriors were carrying them did not necessarily indicate they were hostile. One of the warriors said something in his own tongue, and Smoke Eyes answered him.

"Smoke Eyes, if I'm not welcome, I'll go," Gunn said.

"You are welcome, Gunn," the warrior said, surprising Gunn with his English. "Smoke Eyes has told us that you saved her life. I am Iron Hand, the brother of Smoke Eyes. This is my camp."

"Come," Smoke Eyes said. "It is cold out here. We will go inside where it is warm."

One of the Indians took Esquire and walked him over to their horses, while Gunn followed Smoke Eyes and Iron Hand inside the largest tipi. There was a fire in the center of the tipi, and most of the smoke was drifting up through the hole at the top. But a great deal of it was trapped inside the tipi, and it had already started to burn Gunn's eyes and nose and lungs. He knew that he would grow accustomed to it after a while. Neither Smoke Eyes nor anyone else in the tipi seemed to notice.

Gunn looked around. There was a pale orange glow from the fire, and it was shadowed by the amount of smoke that stayed inside, so that the interior of the tipi was very dim. Despite the dimness, Gunn could see that there were three others in the tipi, including a baby sleeping in a small crib.

"What is this?" Gunn asked, smiling at the baby.

Iron Hand smiled, and sat down, inviting Gunn to do the same thing. The smoke was less bothersome at that level. He accepted a plate of stew put in his hands by Smoke Eyes.

"This is my son, Swift Eagle," Iron Hand said proudly. "He is a fine, strong boy, with a voice as loud as thunder. He will become a mighty hunter."

"Uhmm," Gunn said. "The stew is very good. I thank you for your kindness in sharing it with me."

"Gunn, I have spoken to my brother about O'Toole," Smoke Eyes said.

"O'Toole must be killed," Iron Hand said.

"Yes," Gunn agreed. "I am looking for him now, and when I find him, I will kill him."

"I will tell all of my people that you are to have safe passage through our country," Iron Hand said. "I will tell them to bring you a message if they know where O'Toole is."

"Again, I thank you," Gunn said.

During and after the meal, Gunn and the others talked for a long time. Iron Hand was very interested in the story of the "War Between the White Eyes," as he called the Civil War, and Gunn told him as much about it as he could. It was very difficult for Iron Hand to comprehend the scope of a major battle like Gettysburg, Shiloh, and Missionary Ridge.

"How many were killed in this war?"

"Half a million," Gunn said. Iron Hand didn't understand half a million. "More than every star you can see," Gunn explained. Then he remembered an article he had read in *Harper's Weekly* which explained it more graphically than anything he had ever seen or heard. The average person, the article said, does not come in contact with half a million people within a lifetime. "Iron Hand, if everyone you have ever seen in your life, and if everyone you would ever see, would die, that still wouldn't be as many as were killed in the Civil War."

"I do not understand the white man," Iron Hand said. "The white man must kill everything. The farmer kills all the trees so that he can have an open space. Then he kills the grass by digging up the ground. White men come on the iron horse to kill buffalo, then they get on the iron horse and go away and leave the meat of the buffalo to rot. White men use water to wash away a mountain when they look for the yellow metal, and they kill the mountain and the water. I have been to the towns where the white man makes things from the skins of cows. There is much smoke and bad smell at such places, and the white man kills the air. If the white man kills the ground, where will we stand? If he kills the water, what will we drink? If he kills the air, what will we breathe? If he kills the animals, what will we eat? And if he kills the mountains, where will our spirits go when we die? Sometimes the white man attacks

Indian people in their sleep and they kill the women and the children and the men who have seen too many winter counts to hunt or fight. And sometimes they fight a great war and kill each other, more people than there are stars in the sky. I think the white man will not be happy until everyone and everything is dead."

Gunn didn't answer Iron Hand's indictment. He couldn't.

Finally the fire and the conversation died, and Gunn spread a blanket and robe near the tipi flap. Within a short time he was sound asleep.

When Gunn awoke later that night, he realized that the flap had been drawn back on the tipi to let in fresh air. He looked toward the flap, and saw Smoke Eyes standing in the spill of moonlight.

At first, Gunn couldn't be certain she was naked, because he had only the soft light of the moon in which to see her. Then she turned slightly, and her body was highlighted and made all the more mysterious and intriguing by the subtle shadows and lighting of the night.

Somehow, Smoke Eyes sensed that Gunn was awake, because she turned and walked softly to him. Gunn knew then that she had been waiting for him to wake up.

"I waited for you the last time," Smoke Eyes said. "I waited for you to come to my robes, but you didn't come. If you had come then, it would have been a sign that I would be your woman, and live with you forever. Now, I know that I will not live with you forever. But I can live with you for one night. We will make love tonight."

"Smoke Eyes, your brother and his wife are sleeping here," Gunn cautioned.

"I have listened to them make love many times," Smoke Eyes said. "Now let them hear me."

Smoke Eyes' body was lithe and supple, soft and warm, and she had learned the first time what it took to please him. She knew how to change his blood to liquid fire, to make his cock turn diamond-hard and leak the warm juices.

Gunn started to give her one more excuse why they couldn't . . . why they shouldn't make love, but his excuse died in his throat. Why should he fight it? She was a woman who knew what she wanted, and right now, they definitely wanted the same thing.

Smoke Eyes straddled him, taking him into her, then rocking back and forth in an ever quickening rhythm. It was strongly physical and immensely satisfying, but it was much more than that. It was as if their passions were perfectly orchestrated to move in harmony, so that there was a tremendous sense of mutual need and fulfillment.

After their desires were satisfied, they went back to sleep. Gunn awoke once more in the middle of the night. The moon still shone brightly, sailing high in the velvet sky. It spilled a pool of silvery radiance through the tipi opening and onto the robe-covered ground. Smoke Eyes was breathing softly beside him.

He went back to sleep, still full of her.

Chapter Eleven

In the miner's camp, Lee woke long before dawn. He lay there listening to the roar of the river for a few moments, then realized that they had made a mistake by choosing to camp here. If anyone tried to sneak up on them, their approach would be masked by the sound of the rushing water. It was too late to worry about it now.

Lee shrugged off his blanket and looked at Sam, the one whose time it was to be awake now. Sam was sitting on a rock in the dark, slightly illuminated by the banked coals of the campfire. He was holding his Winchester across his knees, and looking off toward the mountains. Sam glanced around when he heard Lee get up.

"Well, I wondered when you'd wake up. What's the matter? Did someone try 'n steal your money while you was asleep?" Sam asked, stroking his beard.

"What do you mean?" Lee asked.

Sam chuckled. "The way you was a'tossin' around in your blankets, I figured you was either havin' a nightmare 'bout somebody takin' your money, or else you had a woman in there with you. Now you bein'

ıch a fine upstandin' family man that you put me 'n
lay to shame, I knowed you wouldn't be havin' no
oman. So I figured it had to be a nightmare."

"You can't have a nightmare without sleep," Lee
ıid. "And I didn't get no sleep."

"Still worryin' about that stranger that come into
ur camp last night?"

"Yes," Lee admitted. "Didn't you notice his hands?
e ain't never done a lick of work in his life. He
ıeren't no more a prospector than I am a railroad
ıgineer. He was up to no good, I know he was. I just
ɔn't know what he has planned, that's all."

"Maybe he seen there was no way he could take on
ıe three of us," Sam suggested. "Maybe he decided
ʒin doin' anythin'."

Lee walked over to the edge of the little circle and
ɛgan relievin' himself. It made a pattering sound
ʒainst the crust of the snow, and a little cloud of
ıpor floated up. "Listen, Sam, there ain't no sense
ı the both of us goin' without sleep," he called back
ver his shoulder. "If you want, I'll stand the guard."

"Ah, you are a good man, Lee," Sam said. "I was
ɛttin' a mite sleepy." Sam set his weapon down by his
ʌwn sleeping bag, then began to pull off his boots. "I
ıade some fresh coffee 'bout an hour ago," he
ıded, pointing to the pot suspended over the fire.

Lee finished, buttoned up his pants, then turned
ıck toward the center. His nose was running in the
ɔld, morning air, and he wiped it with the back of
s hand. "Thanks," he said with a sniff.

Sam climbed into his own sleeping bag and pulled a
ɹanket up to his shoulders. "Oh, listen," Sam said.
ʟong as you're treatin' me so nice 'n all, how 'bout

havin' breakfast ready when I wake up? Eggs, wit the yellow soft 'n the white hard, ham, biscuits, an some fried taters."

"Sure," Lee laughed. "Glad to oblige. For half you share."

Sam chuckled, and Lee poured himself a cup c coffee, then he sat on the same rock Sam had usec He took a sip and looked out over the hills. They wer great slabs of silver and black under the bright moor It was quiet for several moments and Lee though Sam had already gone to sleep. Then Sam spoke t him.

"Lee?" There was a strange, plaintive quality t Sam's voice, and Lee looked toward him, not at a sure he was awake. "Lee?" Sam said again.

"Yes?"

"Me'n Clay was talkin' 'bout it last night. You bee a good partner. When you go off to Oregon to bu your farm, we're gonna miss you."

Gunn wasn't used to sleeping so close to a bab and when the baby began its morning feeding, it wok Gunn up. Gunn opened his eyes and looked throug the early gray light at the baby's mother as she gav her breast to her child. The mother smiled shyly Gunn, and Gunn smiled back, then looked ove toward Smoke Eyes, who was still asleep.

At moments like this Gunn thought of Laurie, an what might have been. It didn't take too muc imagination to picture his own wife nursing the chil they never had. It would have been nice to wake up i the morning, watch his child be nursed, then g

146

tside to work his ranch. That scene was reality for ousands of ranchers all over the West. It was only atasy for William Gunnison.

Iron Hand got up and walked over to the flap of e tipi. He opened it wide and took his first step ough it when there was an angry snarl, then the pact of a bullet against flesh. A rifle shot echoed om outside, and Iron Hand let out a grunt as he fell ck into the tipi, with blood pumping from his est.

Iron Hand's wife gave a shout of surprise, and sat quickly, pulling her breast from the baby's mouth, o, surprised by the sudden action, began crying. oke Eyes jumped up and started toward the flap ening to see what was going on.

"Down!" Gunn shouted, motioning with his hand. tay down low!"

With the sound of shooting going on all around n, Gunn pulled on his pants and boots. Bullets re popping through the skin of the tipi, and one hit e support pole nearest Gunn, splintering the pole d sending a small sliver, stinging into his arm.

"It is O'Toole!" Smoke Eyes said. "This is how it s before!"

"Not quite how it was before," Gunn answered. he bastards aren't going to ride out without a atch this time."

Gunn tugged on pants and boots, didn't bother to ok for his shirt. Instead, bare chested, he ran out of e tent, carrying his pistol with him. The first thing saw when he stepped outside was a little child nning. Then, with horror, he saw an explosion of ood and brain matter as a bullet crashed into the

147

child's head.

Gunn looked toward a nearby line of trees. Ther he saw three mounted men, firing confidently into t camp. He raised his pistol and fired, and one of the tumbled from his horse. He fired again, and t second one went down. By now the one remaini attacker realized that the odds had turned drastica against him, and he whipped his horse around a started away at a gallop. Gunn fired a third time, b the man, already at the extreme edge of pistol rang quickly put a safe distance between himself a Gunn. Gunn cursed in impotent rage.

"Gunn!" Smoke Eyes shouted, and when Gu looked around, he saw that she was handing him Sharps .52 caliber. Gunn smiled grimly. This was t same type weapon he had seen in Eb's camp. T Sharps was also the weapon used by Berdan's Shar shooters during the war, and stories had been told Berdan's marksmen dropping their targets from d tances of 700 yards.

Gunn walked, almost leisurely, over to lean agair a large rock. It was cold, and the texture of the ro was rough, but he didn't even feel it against his ba skin. Using the rock as a stable aiming platform, took a long, careful bead on the fleeing rider, leadi him just a bit. Slowly, he increased the pressure the trigger until the gun went off. The rifle roare and kicked back against his shoulder. Flame leap out from the breechblock as the linen cartrid burned, and a billowing puff of smoke rolled out the end of the barrel. An instant later the fleei rider, who was four hundred yards away, pitch headfirst from his saddle. His horse, riderless no galloped away.

The Indians gathered around Gunn then, laughing and exhibiting their awe and thanks. Most of them couldn't speak English, and when language failed them, they acted out what he had done by making a pistol with their hands, simulating the killing of the first two, then they took up a rifle to kill the third.

"Never have I seen shooting such as this," one of the Indians who could speak English said. "From this day the nations of the Sioux will call you Shadow Hand, for your hand is fast, and death comes from your fingers. Your enemies must know great fear of you."

"There's one that damn well better fear me," Gunn said. He looked at Smoke Eyes. "How is Iron Hand?"

"My brother is dead," Smoke Eyes said.

"I am sorry, Smoke Eyes."

Gunn looked into the tipi and saw Iron Hand still lying where he had fallen. His wife was beside him weeping quietly.

"I hope your spirit finds those mountains you were talking about," Gunn said softly.

O'Toole, Taylor and Hargis left their horses tied up about two hundred yards away from the miners' camp.

"Listen to that river roar," Taylor said. He laughed. "Those damn fool miners don't have any better sense than to camp by a river like that . . . hell, we could have a brass band with us and still surprise them. They's no way they can hear us comin' over all that."

"Aye," O'Toole said. "But I'll feel a mite better if

149

we're quiet, all the same."

"I wonder how Smitty and Hollifield and Morgan are makin' out with the Indian camp?" Hargis asked.

"What's there to do?" Taylor replied. "Just shoot up a few tipis, is all. They got the easy job, the Indians won't be watchin' for them. These miners is lookin' out for somethin'."

"I can smell the smoke," Hargis said.

"How far?" O'Toole asked.

"If they ain't moved since last night, they're just beyond that clump of trees there," Taylor said.

"All right, lads, from here on in, no more talkin'," O'Toole ordered.

Slowly, O'Toole and his two men moved toward the thicket of trees. When they got to the trees, O'Toole signalled for the others to lie down. For the last few feet, they squirmed forward on their bellies. Then they saw the camp.

Two men were still in their bedrolls. One man was up, and standing at the campfire, pouring himself a cup of coffee. His rifle was leaning against a rock, some ten feet away from where he was.

O'Toole smiled, and raised his rifle to his shoulder. He took a long careful aim, then squeezed off a shot just as the man was raising his coffee cup to his lips. The bullet smashed through the tin cup, then tore into the miner's face, punched through the bone and furrowed up through the soft brain tissue before exiting from the back of his head. The miner died before he ever knew he was in danger.

Hargis and Taylor fired at the two men who were in blankets, and one of them, a man with a beard, sat up and looked around in surprise before a second

ullet crashed through his heart. The other sleeping
man made no move at all as the bullets tore into him.
Not one shot was returned.

"Enough lads, enough," O'Toole said, holding up
his hand. The echo of the last shot rolled back from
the trees and was swallowed up by the roar of the
river. "I'm not one for wastin' ammunition if we've no
need to."

"We don't need to shoot no more, they're dead,"
Taylor said. He stood up and looked toward the
camp. "We killed 'em all."

"Come on!" Hargis shouted, standing up and starting toward the three bodies. "Come on, let's get what
they got on 'em!"

The three walked into the camp and started searching the bodies of the slain miners. O'Toole looked at
the body of the man he had killed. The face of the
dead man was covered with blood, and disfigured by
the bullet, and the piece of tin cup which the impact
of the bullet had driven into the flesh. O'Toole knelt
down beside him and started rifling through his
clothes. He pulled a letter from the man's inner
pocket, then opened the envelope and found a photograph. He studied the photograph in the gray, morning light. The picture was of a woman and a girl. The
girl was about the same age as his own daughter.

When O'Toole thought of his own daughter, his jaw
tightened with anger. His daughter was a conniving
little bitch who had no idea of the concept of respect
or gratitude. He transferred the bitterness he felt for
his own daughter to the sepia image in the photograph, and, with a curse, tossed the picture and the
letter onto the red hot coals. He watched it as it

blackened around the edges, caught fire and curle
up to disappear in a dancing flame and a plume o
smoke.

"Yahoo! Look at this, men! I found it!" Harg
said, and he held up a couple of sacks of gold dus
There were four more on the ground beside him.

"Remember," O'Toole said. "There are three mor
who get a share."

"Yeah, yeah, I'm not forgettin'," Hargis said. "Bu
that's still a bag apiece, and it'll be good enough t
put on a drunk I'll never forget."

"Where to now, Jake?" Taylor asked.

"The others'll be comin' to Deadwood," O'Tool
said. "I told 'em that's where we'd be, 'n that's where
intend to be."

"I know," Taylor said. "But I mean after that
What've you got planned to do next?"

"Next?" O'Toole ran his hand through his hair. "I'n
after thinkin' that our friend Gunn has got to b
attended to before we can get on with our own lives
It's time we tended to him."

The Deadwood stage was right on time as it starte
down the series of cutbacks before reaching its fina
destination. The road came across Bear Butte Pass
three thousand feet above the town, then droppe
right down into Deadwood. Thus it was said by th
stage drivers that they didn't drive into Deadwood
they descended into it. The illusion was furthe
heightened by the fact that Deadwood became visibl
as soon as the stage crested the pass, and remaine
visible, like a toy village in a toy valley, as the stag

wound its way down from the clouds which often clung to the top of the mountain.

Caitlin was a passenger in the coach, and as she rode she peered through the window at the tiny town below, and wondered about the man she had met, ever so briefly, in Mystic. She could still see his broad chest and wide shoulders, and the even, white teeth that smiled at her from the handsome face.

Caitlin's innocence went as far as her virginity. No man had known her, though there were many who would have paid any price for the privilege. Though Caitlin had discouraged any one man from getting too close to her, she did secretly enjoy their attention, and took a measure of pride in the fact that she could arouse such wanting in a man. But always before, it had been a one-sided thing, with the man doing the pursuing, and Caitlin managing to stay just out of their reach.

Now, that was all changed. Ever since the moment she had met Gunn, she had schemed to get him. When she thought of him, and that was often, she experienced a spreading warmth in her body and a weakness in her knees. No man had ever made her feel this way before, and she had no idea what it was about this one that affected her so.

The men Gunn had shot in Mystic were from Deadwood. Caitlin knew that one of them, Sorghum, had encountered Gunn in Deadwood before their fatal meeting in Mystic, so she took a chance that Gunn would be in Deadwood. If not, then she expected him to show up. When he did show up, she wanted to be there.

Caitlin leaned her head back in the stage and

closed her eyes. When she did so, a picture came to her. It was the picture of a sixteen-year-old girl, comforting her mother.

"Why do you stay with him, Mama?" she asked as she dabbed lightly with a wet cloth at her mother's cut and swollen lips.

"Because he is my husband, Caitlin. And he's your papa."

"I hate him," Caitlin said.

"Oh, child, you mustn't hate your papa. That's a sin. The Fifth Commandment says; 'Honor thy mother and thy father.' You must love him."

"I love you, Mama," Caitlin said. "I honor you. But I can never love a man who beats you the way he does, and I don't know how you can."

"It's . . . it's not so bad," the woman said.

"I'm afraid, Mama," Caitlin said.

"What are you afraid of?"

"I'm afraid that someday he might hurt you so bad that . . . that . . ." Caitlin couldn't go on.

"Caitlin, if that ever happens, you must promise me something," Caitlin's mother said.

"What?"

"You must promise that you won't do anything."

"Do anything? What do you mean, do anything?"

"You know what I mean, Caitlin," her mother said. "You are a strong-willed girl, and you have some of your papa's temper."

"I hope I don't have anything of his," Caitlin said.

"You're his daughter, dear. Of course you have something of his. You have his temper but not his . . . his evil ways. And you'll never have his evil ways unless you give in to them, unless you act as he would

154

ct. That's why I want you to promise me that if anything happens to me, you won't seek revenge."

"Mama, you're frightening me."

"I'm sorry. I don't intend to frighten you. And I'm sure nothing ever will happen. But, darling, your father is a powerful man, with a violent temper. And sometimes when he's been drinking, he does things that he doesn't mean. I know he doesn't mean them. And if, one day, he . . . he did do something that he didn't mean, and if I would . . . die, I want you to promise me that you won't do anything."

"Mama, I can't promise you that."

"Promise me, Caitlin. If you love me . . ."

"Of course I love you!" Caitlin said quickly.

"Then you must promise me. You won't try to do anything to your papa."

"I . . . I promise," Caitlin said.

Exactly two months after Caitlin made that promise to her mother, her father came home in a drunken rage and began beating her mother. He beat her into insensibility, and this time, despite all Caitlin's nursing and loving care, her mother didn't recover.

When her mother died, Caitlin loaded up a Navy Colt and waited for her father to come home. She stood in the pitch black under the stairs, and when he was fumbling around in the dark, trying to light a lantern, she raised the pistol and pointed it at him. She was at point-blank range, and, with the slightest twitch on the trigger, she could have blown the top of his head off.

Just before she pulled the trigger, the image of her mother popped back into her head, and she heard herself making the promise to her mother. She had

155

never wanted anything as badly in her life, as she wanted to kill her father at that moment. But she couldn't violate the oath she had given her mother.

Caitlin sighed, and lowered the pistol. When her father stumbled off to bed a few moments later, Caitlin hurried to her room, threw a few things in a bag, then left home.

Caitlin had been taught to sew by her mother, and that skill came in handy when she got out on her own. No matter where she wound up, she could always find a job as a seamstress. She had worked in Denver, Cheyenne, Laramie, Rapid City and Mystic. She imagined she could work just as well in Deadwood.

Caitlin heard the stage driver blow his horn to alert the people that he was coming into town, and the bleat of his trumpet brought her out of her reverie. She looked through the window and smiled as the stage rolled down the main street of Deadwood. Her smile left her face when the stage stopped in front of the Deadwood saloon.

There, standing on the front porch of the saloon, she saw her father, Jacob O'Toole.

Chapter Twelve

Though the others in the coach were exiting through the door that faced the Deadwood Saloon, Caitlin slid across the seat to step out on the street side. She stood in the middle of the street and looked toward the top of the stage, while the driver searched through the luggage, selecting the individual bags of the passengers who were disembarking here.

"Driver," Caitlin said as quietly as possible.

The driver looked around.

"The brown carpet bag is mine."

"Lo', Miss, what are you doin' standin' out there in the street?" the driver asked. "I pulled close enough to the porch here that you could'a stepped out without so much as dirtyin' your feet."

"Please," Caitlin said.

"I'll get your bag, Miss," the driver said. "It just don't make no sense, that's all."

The driver's voice was loud and curious, and it undid what Caitlin was trying to do. She had exited on the street side so she could avoid her father. But her father, drawn by the driver's words, stepped down from the porch and walked around behind the stage. He stood with his hand resting lightly on the boot, and saw his daughter waiting for the driver to hand down the bag. As the driver found the bag and started to pass it down, O'Toole reached for it.

"Sure'n you'd better let me get it for you, my darlin'," he said. " 'Tis a might heavy for a wee slip of a girl."

"I'm not a 'wee slip of a girl', and I'm not your darlin'," Caitlin said, taking the bag before O'Toole could get it."

"Of course you're my darlin'," O'Toole said. "You're my daughter, aren't you?"

"No," Caitlin said resolutely. "I stopped being your daughter two years ago."

"Ah, I see," O'Toole said. "So you'd still be blamin' me for your poor mother dyin' like she done. I'd hoped you'd be over that by now."

"I'll get over that, when Mama gets over being dead," Caitlin retorted sharply.

"Darlin', if you're honest with yourself, you'll be knowin' that you never gave me a chance to explain what really happened," O'Toole said. "You just ran out on me without so much as a by your leave."

"I promised Mama I wouldn't kill you," Caitlin said. "That was the chance I gave you."

" 'Tis about supper time," O'Toole said. "Have supper with me, and be of kind enough heart to listen to my side. If you don't change your mind about me, I'll be more'n glad to go my way 'n you'll never see nor hear from me again."

"Is that a promise?"

"Aye, lass, 'n I'll make the same on the Good Book if you wish."

"I don't think you'd recognize the Good Book if you saw it," Caitlin said. She sighed. "All right. I'll listen to your side, just this once."

O'Toole handed Caitlin's carpet bag to a man and ordered that it be taken to the hotel, then he took her to Kate's Place for supper.

The dining room of Kate's Place was warm and full of good smells. There were a dozen or so diners at the tables scattered around the room, all of them eating heartily of the fare before them. There were some tables with dirty dishes still on them, evidence of diners recently left, and there was one table near the back which was clean. They headed for that table.

"Be right with you," Kate called to them as she walked by with her arms loaded with full supper plates.

" 'Tisn't a fancy place," O'Toole said. "But the food's as good as you get in Deadwood."

"You were the only one in the family ever worried about fancy places," Caitlin said.

"Ah, you're still holdin' an anger in your heart," O'Toole said. "And you've not even heard my side, yet."

"All right . . . Father," Caitlin said, and she set the word 'Father' apart from the rest of the sentence, as if it were something distasteful, even to say. "What is your side?"

"Darlin', what do you know of laudanum?"

"Laudanum? The medicine?"

"Aye, the medicine," O'Toole said. "But 'tis much more than medicine. It's a witch's brew, stronger and more evil than any whiskey on God's earth. When a little is taken, for pain, 'tis all right. But sometimes a body gets to needin' it, 'n they take more'n more until it's their whole life . . . it's all they think about. Oh, believe me, lass, no one captured by demon rum has ever suffered like a body who has need of laudanum."

"I don't understand," Caitlin said. "What has that to do with Mama?"

"Some years back, your mama took ill with headaches. These were no ordinary headaches, girl, these were pains the likes of which you can't imagine. Your poor mama suffered so that it wrenched my heart to think of it." O'Toole sighed, and looked at the table before him. "Here I'm tellin' you this story so's you won't hold me guilty anymore, but the truth is, lass, you can't begin to hold me as guilty as I hold myself. For you see, in tryin' to relieve your poor mama's sufferin', 'twas me who got her started on laudanum. I would bring her some for her headaches, but she would need more, and the more I would bring her, the more she would need. Finally I realized what was happenin', and I tried to stop her. I wouldn't bring her any more. But that didn't stop her, and that's when she began to . . . to do things."

"Do what sort of things?"

O'Toole put his hand across the table and laid it on Caitlin's.

"She starting seein' other men . . . selling herself to them for enough money to buy laudanum."

"What?" Caitlin gasped, jerking her hand back. "I

160

don't believe that!"

"I know, 'twas hard for me to believe it too," he said. "But we mustn't blame your mama, it wasn't her doin' those things, it was the laudanum doin' it."

"All right, suppose that is true . . . and I'm not saying I believe it," Caitlin said. "But, suppose it is true. If the laudanum was making her do those things, why did you beat her?"

"That's just it, lass," O'Toole said. "I didn't beat her. 'Twas the men she took up with who beat her. She let on to you and to a few others that it was me beatin' her, 'n because I didn't want to expose her to the shame of ever'one knowin' the real truth, I let her tell her tales. The night she died, she had been badly beaten by a drunken cowboy. Even then, she said it was me that beat her, 'n I let her say it, never knowin' she so beaten that she would die . . . 'n never knowin' that it would cost me the only thing in this world that ever mattered to me . . . my own, darlin' daughter."

O'Toole blinked a couple of times, and Caitlin believed she could see a sheen of tears in his eyes. She was flabbergasted. Was her father telling the truth? If so, she had wronged him, wronged him terribly.

"Papa," she finally said. "I don't know if you are telling me the truth or lying to me. If you are telling the truth, then I'm going to owe you a big apology. But if you're lying to me, then the fires of hell won't be hot enough to punish you for all your sins."

Smitty and the others had been surprised when somebody suddenly popped out of one of the tipis and began returning their fire. They had expected no more trouble than on any of their other attacks against isolated Indian camps. But after only a few shots at the tipis, a white man appeared with his gun blazing.

Smitty was the first to go down. Hollifield second. Smitty was gutshot, and while he was lying on the ground in pain, he saw Hollifield take a bullet right between the eyes. Even as Hollifield was going down, Morgan broke and ran.

"Morgan! Don't leave me, Morgan!" Smitty had screamed, but Morgan, bent upon saving his own life, paid absolutely no attention to Smitty's shout for help.

The white man was Gunn. Smitty discovered that fact when he heard the Indian girl call him by name as she handed him the Sharps rifle. Smitty saw Gunn lean against the rock and take a long, steady aim, and he knew that Morgan was as good as dead. Smitty watched, almost disinterestedly, as the big rifle roared and kicked back against Gunn's shoulder. He saw Morgan go down, and he was glad Gunn had killed the son of a bitch. It served him right for running out on him.

There was a lot of underbrush and rocks where Smitty fell, and, using that as concealment, he managed to crawl away. On the other side of the ridgeline, he found his horse just standing quietly, reins hanging straight down to the ground.

"Good horse," Smitty said, crawling toward him. "Good horse."

His horse was spooked by the smell of blood, and

by the fact that his owner was crawling toward him, rather than approaching him upright, as he normally did. The horse whickered, and stamped his feet in confusion. Smitty was afraid that he might be stomped, but finally, he got hold of the reins and calmed his animal down.

"Good horse," he said again.

Smitty pulled himself, painfully, into the saddle, then started away, walking his horse at first so that Gunn and the Indians wouldn't hear him. When he thought he was far enough away, he broke into a gallop in order to open as much distance as he could between Gunn and himself.

Smitty headed for the hideout. He stopped several times to put moss on his wound, but he had no idea if that was really helping. The bleeding stopped, but Smitty didn't know if that was a good sign or bad. Maybe it stopped because he didn't have any more blood.

A couple of times, Smitty found himself on the ground, and he couldn't remember how he got there. He didn't know if he had dismounted to rest, or if he had fallen off his horse. Every time he would discover himself on the ground, however, he would summon the strength to get back on his horse and resume his ride. He knew he had to make it to the hideout before nightfall. If he had to stay outside tonight with this wound, he would freeze to death. He didn't want to die out in the woods like some wounded animal.

Eventually, the terrible pain stopped and a warming numbness set in. It was that numbness that allowed Smitty to go on. But with the numbness came also a weakness from loss of blood, and by the time Smitty reached the cabin O'Toole used for a hideout, he was staying on his horse only by supreme effort of will.

Holding on to the pommel of his saddle, Smitty rode the last few hundred yards toward the low, log cabin, set back against the base of a rock cliff. A golden square of light shone its welcome through the window, and a wisp of wood smoke rose from the chimney, carrying with it the aroma of frying meat. Someone was here, and they were having their supper. Smitty smiled. What a surprise guest he was going to make.

Smitty pulled his pistol out and shot once, waited for a few seconds, then shot two more times. That was the prescribed signal for anyone approaching the cabin. The cabin door opened almost immediately, and he saw Taylor step out onto the front porch.

"Who is it?" Taylor called.

"It's me, Smitty. I got myself a little gutshot this mornin'," he said, laughing weakly.

Smitty felt himself beginning to weave about, then he pitched out of the saddle. He passed out when he hit the ground.

Smitty was warm when he opened his eyes. He saw that he was lying in a bunk near the stove. Taylor and Hargis were sitting at a table eating their supper.

"Taylor?" Smitty called.

Taylor got up and walked over to the bunk to look down on Smitty.

"Yeah, what do you want?"

"Did you send for a doctor?"

Taylor was eating a sandwich, and he took a bite, then wiped the back of his hand across his mouth.

"What the hell would I want to send for a doctor for? You know O'Toole would kill me if I let anyone know where this place is. Besides, you're gutshot, boy. You're gonna die anyway . . . probably before mornin'."

"No," Smitty said. "I'm better now, I know I am. I don't hurt as much as I did."

"That just proves you're dyin'," Taylor said. "Hell, don't it make sense to you that you ought to be hurtin' with a bullet in your belly?"

"Taylor, I don't want to die."

"It's your own damn fault," Taylor said. "You ain't got no better sense than to let yourself get kilt by a bunch of Indian squaws 'n kids."

"It was Gunn," Smitty said.

Taylor stopped with his sandwich half-way to his mouth.

"Gunn?"

"Yeah. He was there with them. You know the Indian girl he was with at the Proxmire camp? Well, he was still with her."

"Son of a bitch," Taylor swore. "Will we never get that bastard out of our hair?"

"You sure it was Gunn?" Hargis asked.

"Yeah, I'm sure," Smitty said. "I heard the Indian girl call him that. He come out of the tipi half naked, blazing away with a six-shooter. He got me with the first shot, hit Hollifield right between the eyes with his second. It was the best pistol shot I ever seen. Then he used a rifle to drop Morgan when he was a

165

quarter of a mile away."

"We gotta tell O'Toole," Taylor said. "We gotta go in and tell him now . . . tonight."

"What about me?" Smitty asked. "Taylor, you ain't gonna leave me out here to die, are you?"

"You got your choice," Taylor said. "You can die quick or slow. Which will it be?"

"You ain't leavin' me, you son of a bitch!" Smitty shouted, and he started clawing for his gun.

Smitty had never been fast with a gun. Now, lying on his back, and slowed by fatigue and weakness, he was pitifully slow in getting his weapon out. Taylor drew, almost leisurely, and shot Smitty in the head. The sound of Taylor's gunshot was deafening inside the small cabin, and a thick blue cloud of smoke drifted through the room.

Hargis walked over to the bunk and looked at the open, sightless eyes of the man who had once ridden with them.

"I guess he wanted to die quick," Hargis said with a chuckle.

"Come on," Taylor said. "Let's get him outside and buried, then go see O'Toole. He's gonna have to take care of Gunn, one way or the other, or that son of a bitch is gonna wind up killin' us all."

Could Caitlin have been wrong about her father all this time? Was it really as he said it was? Was he taking the blame for something he didn't do?

She wanted to believe him; after all, he was her father. But there were too many things that still

166

needed explaining before she was able to totally believe him. And one thing that she could never believe, was that her mother had sold herself to men.

Just as Caitlin and her father were finished their supper, two men came into the cafe to talk to him. They seemed highly agitated about something.

"What are you doin' here? I thought you were at Cottonwood Canyon."

"Jake, we gotta talk to you," one of them said.

"Lads, I want you to meet my own darlin' daughter," O'Toole said. "She left me some time ago, 'n like the prodigal son, now she's returned."

"It's important, Jake. It's real important."

"Well now, I'm sure 'tis important. But can it be more important than my own daughter, now?"

"It's about . . ."

O'Toole held up his hand to stop him in midsentence.

"We'll be talkin' out on the front porch," he said. "I'll not be disturbin' my daughter's peace with your news."

"Papa, I want to check into the hotel anyway," Caitlin said. "I've had a tiring trip. Besides, I want to think about a few things."

"Do that, daughter, do that," O'Toole said, as he walked as far as the front porch with her. "And we'll be havin' breakfast together."

Once on the front porch, Caitlin nodded at the two men who were still anxiously waiting to talk to her father, then started down the sidewalk toward the hotel.

"Now, what is it?" O'Toole asked, as Caitlin was

leaving.

"It's Gunn. He's showed up again," Taylor said.

"Yeah, he killed Smitty," Hargis added, conveniently forgetting that in fact, Taylor had killed Smitty.

"And Hollifield and Morgan," Taylor said.

"We got to do somethin' about him, Jake. We got to stop him, some way."

"How would you be knowin' all this?" O'Toole asked.

"Smitty told us," Hargis said. "He showed up at the cabin before he died."

"What are we gonna do, Jake?" Taylor asked. "I don't mind tellin' you, I'm scared."

"You gotta come up with somethin'," Hargis said.

"All right, all right, I'll think of somethin'," O'Toole promised, stroking his chin.

"Yeah, well it better be good, 'cause he's tricky as a damn fox," Taylor said.

Suddenly O'Toole grinned broadly. "A fox? Aye, a fox," he said. "Taylor, you've come up with it."

"I've come up with it? I've come up with what? I don't have the slightest idea of what you're talkin' about."

"Tell me, lad, how would you be goin' about catchin' a fox?" O'Toole asked. "You'd trap him, am I right?"

"Yeah, I guess so," Taylor answered, still not aware of where O'Toole was going with this line of reasoning.

"And, in order to set a trap, you've got to have some bait. Well, lads, I've just come up with some bait that'll trap our fox."

"What sort of bait?"

"My daughter," O'Toole said.

"Your daughter?"

"Aye. It seems my daughter met Mr. Gunn on the night he dispatched Sorghum and the others. He made quite an impression on her . . . so much so that she told me all about him over supper tonight."

"So?"

"So, if Gunn made an impression on my daughter, then you can be sure Caitlin made an impression on Gunn. You do think she's a pretty enough lass?"

"Well, yeah, sure," Taylor said, not wanting to disagree with O'Toole.

"Well, then, 'tis really quite simple. Caitlin told me she came to Deadwood hoping to meet Mr. Gunn again, and she's a resourceful enough lass that I'm sure she'll do just that. We'll wait until after they've struck up a friendship . . . then you snatch the girl and take her to the hideout, making sure you leave tracks so he can find you. When he comes after her, you can kill him."

"You want us to snatch your own daughter?"

"Aye. She's perfect for our purpose."

"What if she don't go along with it?" Hargis asked.

"Take her anyway. If we're gonna make it look real, it can't look like she's in on it." O'Toole said. "Now, stay low until after Gunn returns to town. He's got to have time to sniff out the bait."

"Jake, they's one thing I've noticed about baitin' a trap," Taylor observed.

"And what would that be?" O'Toole replied.

"I've noticed that purt' near ever' time the trap gets

169

sprung, the bait gets kilt."

"Aye, that's a fact," O'Toole said.

"Well, we're baitin' this here trap with your own daughter."

"Aye, that we are, that we are," O'Toole said. "But if it'll get rid of Gunn, it's a risk I'm willin' to take."

Chapter Thirteen

Caitlin didn't know how long she had been asleep when something awakened her. It may have been a noise, though as she lay in bed listening, she heard nothing. She had almost decided that it was only a dream and had closed her eyes to go back to sleep when she heard a distinct sound. It was a woman's voice, and the woman had cried out. But there was something strange about the cry. It wasn't a cry of fear or pain. It was a cry unlike anything Caitlin had ever heard before and yet, though it was new to her, she realized instinctively that it was a cry of passion and pleasure.

The sound had a disquieting effect on Caitlin, and she turned over, hoping to find a position that would blot out the sound. When she did turn over she made an amazing discovery. Caitlin gasped as she saw, reflected in the propped-open transom glass above her door, the very thing that had caused the cry of passion. By some optical trick Caitlin's transom was picking up the reflection of the transom across the hallway. As clearly as if she were looking in a mirror, Caitlin could see into the room across the way, where the lamp was burning brightly and a scene of passion was being played out upon the bed. Caitlin was, by chance, thrust into the role of unwitting witness to a secret rite of desire between a man and a woman.

Caitlin could see as clearly as if she were actually in the room with them. She could hear as well, for neither of the two lovers made any effort to be quiet. The bed covering had been cast aside, and two naked figures were clearly visible on the bed. The woman lay with her legs wantonly spread, and Caitlin could see a dark tangle of hair and a pink, glistening cleft. And, for the first time in her life, she saw the imposing sight of a fully aroused man.

The two naked bodies came together on the bed, kissing each other with a strange mixture of tenderness and savage fury.

Caitlin felt bewilderingly alive, and an unusual warmth began to spread through her. She reached up above her head to grab the bedpost as the kisses led to more, and the couple actually came together. She saw then for the first time what actually went on between a man and a woman. And yet, though she could see the couple's frenzied thrashing, some of the wonder remained. Was there pain mixed with what was obviously pleasurable? Was all lovemaking so savage, or was it just the actions of these two? As Caitlin contemplated these things, her own breath began coming in gasps as short and desperate as the breathing of the man and woman on the bed in the other room.

Caitlin was puzzled by the heat she felt. A moment before it had been cool enough for her to require a blanket. Now she cast the blanket aside because she was swept by such heat that she began to perspire. Her sleeping gown had worked its way up her legs, and she felt an unaccustomed breath of air on her bare legs, though the breeze did little to cool the heat which now blazed unchecked in her loins.

Steadily the moans of the man and woman grew louder and more urgent, while their thrashing became more frenzied. They seemed to reach an apex of some sort, a pinnacle which brought louder and more intense little cries and grunts from both of them. Then, strangely, there was a prolonged stillness, and the two lay in each other's arms. Caitlin, who was alone in her own bed, felt a devastating sense of emptiness at that moment. She wished she had not been a witness to the scene. Despite that wish, she was much too absorbed to turn away, even now, when it was finished.

After a few moments, the man rolled away from the woman, and Caitlin was fascinated by the difference in his appearance now from a few moments earlier. Before, he had been almost frightening with the urgent erect thrust of his manhood. Now it wasn't frightening at all, though it was just as intriguing.

The man began pulling on his pants, but the woman continued to lie on the bed with her eyes closed and a soft smile playing across her mouth. She made no effort whatever to cover her nudity. Caitlin was surprised to see the man put some money on the girl's breasts.

"You're a sweet girl," the man's voice said, muffled by the walls but easily understandable.

"Thanks," the woman replied. "Anytime you want me, I'm available."

"As long as I got the money, you mean?" the man asked with a chuckle.

"Honey, you know good lovin' don't come cheap," the woman replied.

"Oh, I know that," the man said. "Yes, ma'am. I know that." The man moved out of sight of the transom, then Caitlin heard the door to the room open and close, followed by the sound of his footsteps retreating down the carpeted hall.

So, Caitlin thought. She had been watching a prostitute. This was what her father said her mother had become. At that moment, Caitlin knew that her father had been lying to her. And if he lied about that, he lied about everything else as well.

After several more minutes, Caitlin was finally able to drift back to sleep. She dreamed about the scene of passion she had witnessed in the room across the hall. But in the dream the scene had undergone a subtle change. She didn't see the prostitute in the bed, she was herself. And it wasn't the strange man, it was Gunn.

The sun had been up for the better part of an hour the next morning, when Gunn stopped Esquire in front of the livery stable. He swung out of the saddle just as Harry Weiner came out to meet him.

"Hello, Gunn," Weiner said, taking the reins to Esquire.

"Weiner," Gunn replied. "Is Jake O'Toole in town?"

"He was yesterday. Ain't seen 'im this mornin'. You want me to tell 'im you're lookin' for 'im?"

"I have a feeling he already knows," Gunn said.

"Will you be goin' back out soon?"

"I don't plan to. I'm going to get some breakfast and take a bath."

"Then you'll be wantin' oats and a rubdown for your horse."

"Yes," Gunn answered. He stretched to work the kinks out from the night he spent on the ground.

"You know you're gettin' yourself quite a reputation around town," Weiner said as he worked to get Esquire's saddle off. "Yes, sir," he went on. "Quite a reputation. Folks say you done single-handed, wiped out most of O'Toole's men."

"Is that what folks say?"

"Indeed it is, indeed it is," Weiner said. "They's some that don't believe it, but when I tell 'em what I seen of you that mornin' you put three of 'em down, why, they believe it then. You're makin' yourself into a famous man."

"Weiner?"

"Yes, Mr. Gunn?"

"I'm not out to build a reputation," Gunn said.

"No, sir, I know you ain't," Weiner said. "Was just talkin', that's all."

"I'm going to Kate's Place for breakfast," Gunn said. "If O'Toole should happen to ask about me, I'm not tryin' to keep it a secret."

"Yes, sir, I'll spread the word," Weiner promised.

Weiner was right, Gunn was building a reputation around town. He noticed it as he walked along the boardwalk heading for Kate's Place. No one wanted to stay on the same side of the street with him, and as he approached, they would all move quickly to the opposite sides of the street, the women showing their disdain by pointedly ignoring him, while the men either nodded, or touched their hats in salute.

Gunn didn't like it when people treated him like that. It set him apart from everyone else, making him an object of attention, and he had no wish to be the object of anyone's curiosity. That was the least of his problems, however. What this type of fame also did was make him a target, not only for O'Toole and his henchmen, but for anyone else who had a hankering for the bounty O'Toole had put up, and a desire to build a reputation of their own. And Gunn knew that whoever killed him would become instantly famous.

Gunn pushed his way into Kate's Place, to be assailed once again by the familiar and pleasant aromas of her kitchen. He looked around the room before he ventured further into it, and saw the beautiful, flame-haired girl he had seen in Mystic. She was the one whose room he had used on the night some of O'Toole's men tried to ambush him.

The girl saw Gunn almost as quickly as he saw her, and she smiled prettily and stood up.

"Mr. Gunn," she said. "What a pleasant surprise to see you again. Won't you join me for breakfast?"

"Well, I don't know," Gunn said. Gunn thought of O'Toole. If O'Toole wanted to shoot him in this cafe is morning, the fact that he was sitting with a young oman wouldn't stop him. That meant that he would e putting this girl in danger if he accepted her vitation. "I hate to be an imposition, Miss . . ." he alized then that he didn't know her last name. She ad introduced herself only as Caitlin.

"O'Toole," the girl said. "Caitlin O'Toole."

Gunn blinked. "O'Toole?"

"Yes," Caitlin smiled. "Well, my hair is red, my es are green, you didn't think I'd be named some-ing like Gonzales, did you?"

"No," Gunn said. "I guess not. Uh, are you kin to ke O'Toole?"

"He's my father," Caitlin said. She looked toward e door. "It's funny, he should've been here by now. he last thing he said to me last night was that we ould have breakfast together."

Gunn smiled. So, O'Toole was going to come here r breakfast. That put the picture in an entirely ifferent light.

"I'd be glad to have breakfast with you," Gunn id, walking over to her table. "I've been wanting to lk to your father."

"Good, good," Caitlin said.

For a while, Gunn harbored the suspicion that aitlin was setting him up, and his every muscle was nsed and alert for whatever might happen. After alf an hour of conversation, however, Gunn came to e conclusion that, not only was Caitlin not setting im up, she was totally unaware of what was going on etween Gunn and her father. He believed that she ight not even know the type of business her father

177

was in.

"You talk as if you don't see your father tha[t] much," Gunn said after a few minutes.

"I don't," Caitlin admitted. "I left home a few year[s] . . . I've been on my own since then. I just happene[d] to run across my father yesterday. It was the first tim[e] I'd seen him in a couple of years. I don't know what[']s keeping him, but I'm hungry. I think we shouldn[']t wait any longer."

"All right," Gunn admitted. He gave Kate the[ir] order, then he and Caitlin resumed their convers[a-] tion.

"Mr. Gunn," Caitlin started.

"Just Gunn," Gunn corrected.

"All right, Gunn," Caitlin said. She smiled at him[.] "I didn't just happen to come to Deadwood. I cam[e] because of you."

"Because of me?"

"Yes. I know it's awful and terribly forward of m[e] but, ever since that night you were in my room[,] you've been on my mind."

Gunn looked into the young girl's cool, green eye[s] and he saw something wanton and naked, like littl[e] red lights, way down at the bottom.

Gunn coughed to cover his embarrassment. H[e] could be cool under fire, but when a young beautif[ul] girl began to show such interest in him, he had [a] difficult time coping with the situation.

"Uh, listen, Caitlin, I'd better be going," he sai[d.] "I've enjoyed the breakfast."

"I will see you again, won't I?" Caitlin asked.

"I'm sure you will," Gunn answered.

178

Half an hour later, Gunn was standing in the hotel
throom watching as the soap bubbles formed when
e last bucket of hot water was poured into the
ormous bathtub. He paid the boy who had carried
e water up for him, locked the door, then un-
essed. Then just as he stepped into the water, the
or opened. Gunn looked around in surprise. There
od Caitlin O'Toole.

"What are you doing here?" Gunn asked.

Caitlin had prepared a flip remark, such as, 'now
u know what it's like to be surprised by having
meone come in on you', but she was unable to
eak. Instead she stood there for a moment, mes-
erized by the sight of Gunn's muscular, nude body,
ining now with the sheen of moisture collected
om the steaming water.

"I . . . I just came in for a bath," Caitlin said,
eakly.

"How? The door was locked."

"I know," Caitlin said. She took a deep breath and
mmoned again the courage which had allowed her
come in the first place. She held up a key. "I gave
e bellboy two dollars for the key." Caitlin began
king off her clothes.

"What are you doing?" Gunn asked.

"I told you, I came in for a bath. I want to take a
th with you," Caitlin said. She pointed to the tub.
s you can see, it's clearly big enough for both of us
use at the same time."

"Caitlin," Gunn said, and even as he spoke, he

179

could feel the rising tide of his own arousal. "Caitl
I think you'd better leave."

By now Caitlin was down to her chemise, and
she began opening the fastenings, she exposed h
breasts. One nipple peeked through, winking
Gunn, and he knew then that it had already reach
the point that he didn't really want her to leave.

"Gunn, last night I saw a man and woman maki
love," Caitlin said in a voice which was husky w
desire. "I had never witnessed such a thing befo
I've never done it, you know . . . never been wit
man. But I knew when I was watching them tha
wanted to be with you. I want you, Gunn. I want y
to make love to me."

"Caitlin, you're young, you're a virgin, you sho
think twice before you do something like this."

"Oh, I've thought twice, ten times, a hundr
times," Caitlin said. "As a matter of fact, that's al
do think about. I'm burning up inside, and i
because I want you."

Caitlin stepped into the bathtub with Gunn, th
sat down, pulling Gunn down with her. They we
facing each other from opposite ends of the tub, a
some of the soap bubbles moved up to adorn, but r
conceal, Caitlin's beautiful breasts.

Gunn raised his hands to her breasts and gen
caressed the soap-slickened nipple.

"Oh," she said, shivering as he touched her. "I wa
to touch you, too." Gunn felt her hand under water
she wrapped her fingers around his cock. She gaspe
"It's . . . wonderful," she breathed unable to think
any other words to describe what she was feelin

180

While they were bathing, Gunn noticed that he was gradually able to see more and more of her body as the suds began to disappear. Each minute after tantalizing minute, she was more open to his view until finally every soap bubble was gone and he could see the red spate of hair at the junction of her legs, darkened by the water, but still flaming in color.

Caitlin moved toward Gunn, then slipped up onto his legs and slid toward him until his swollen penis was at the opening of her boiling hot tunnel. She spread her legs wider, opening to allow him entry, then guided him just inside. He reached around behind her, putting his hands on her buttocks to pull her toward him. She was well oiled with the fluid of her desire, and that, as well as her own eagerness, allowed him to slide easily into her, until he reached the barrier of her virginity. There he was stopped.

"No," she whimpered. "No, don't stop now. Don't stop."

"It might hurt a little." Gunn warned her.

"I want it to hurt a little. I want to feel it, to remember it when you go deep inside." Caitlin tried to slide forward, to force it herself, but she didn't have the strength to do it. "Oh, please!" she begged. "Do it!"

Gunn pulled her forward sharply, feeling it break as he slipped deep, deep inside.

"Oh . . . God!" Caitlin shouted, and Gunn knew that it wasn't from pain that she called out. She had orgasmed at that very moment, and he could feel her muscles squeeze his cock, squeezing and sucking and drawing at it until he felt a tiny dissolving begin in the middle of his back. He held it in check for a moment.

"More," Caitlin said. "Oh, I want more." She slid up and down on him now, taking him deep inside, then rising up so that he was almost out, then dropping down on him to take him inside again. Her red hair flew wildly across her face, her breasts bounced and rubbed against him, her loins smacked into his as she moved up and down on him, a thrashing, writhing, quivering mass of white-hot flesh.

Suddenly Caitlin threw her arms around Gunn's neck and kissed him, thrusting her tongue deep into his mouth to drown out her own moans as she climaxed again, and this time Gunn was unable to hold in check the dissolving feeling which began deep inside. The tingling sensation boiled into his scrotum, rushed up into his cock, then exploded, spraying his hot seed deep into her womb.

Gunn returned to his room for a nap, and he had been asleep a couple of hours when a loud knock on his door woke him up. He lay there for a moment, wondering why he was asleep in the middle of the day, then he remembered where he was. The knock came a second time, louder than before, and he reached for his pistol.

"Who is it?" Gunn called.

"Mr. Gunn? Mr. Gunn, it's me, Harry Weiner."

Weiner. The liveryman.

"Is something wrong with Esquire?" Gunn asked, jumping out of bed and moving quickly to the door.

He jerked it open and saw Weiner standing just out in the hall.

"No, there's nothing wrong with your horse," Weiner said.

"Then what is it? Why did you wake me?"

"It's the girl, Mr. Gunn. The girl you ate breakfast with this mornin', remember?"

"Yes, of course I remember. What about her?"

"Well sir, she was took by Taylor and Hargis," Weiner said. "They're a couple of O'Toole's men. Fact is, they are the only two he's got left."

"Took by them? What do you mean, took by them?"

"They took 'er with 'im," Weiner said. "And they sent you a message. You're to come to Cottonwood Canyon if you don't want anythin' to happen to the girl."

"That's the message they gave you to tell me?"

"Yes, sir."

Gunn sighed and walked back into his room where he sat on the bed and began pulling on his boots. "Well," he said. "I'm glad to know where Taylor and Hargis are, but I wouldn't worry about the girl if I were you. She's probably in on it, she's O'Toole's daughter."

"Lord, that don't mean nothin', Mr. Gunn," Weiner said. "Ever'one in town knows that O'Toole kilt his own wife by beatin' her to death. If he'd do that to his wife, why, he'd just as likely do it to his daughter. Besides, she didn't look to me like she was in on it. They'd done beat her up pretty good. Her eyes was black 'n her mouth was all cut 'n bleedin'. If you

183

don't come out there, I think they mean to kill he
Mr. Gunn. Fact is, I think they mean to kill he
whether you come out there or not."

"What about O'Toole? Was he with them?"

"I didn't see him," Weiner said.

"All right, first things first," Gunn answered. "I'
take care of O'Toole later. Now, tell me how to fin
Cottonwood Canyon."

Gunn cursed under his breath. He knew the odd:
O'Toole now held all the cards.

He knew that if he rode to Cottonwood Canyon, h
was probably riding to his own death.

Chapter Fourteen

It took Gunn an hour and a half of hard riding to reach the upper rim of Cottonwood Canyon. He got off Esquire to give the Tennessee Walker a much needed breather, then walked out to the edge to look over. The canyon was at least six hundred feet deep, and below him, the North Fork Rapid creek resembled a green snake stretched out across the canyon floor. The green was from the vegetation which grew alongside the creekbank. The creek itself was a small, brown line scratched through the middle of the green.

Six hundred feet straight down below him was the cabin hideout used by O'Toole and his gang. It was from here that O'Toole had launched his murderous raids against peaceful Indians and helpless miners. And it was here that O'Toole had stooped to the low of using his own daughter as a hostage. From up here, the cabin looked like a tiny box, and Gunn could just about drop a rock on the roof.

Weiner had explained to Gunn that there was onl[y] one trail into the canyon, and that was what made th[e] canyon such an ideal hideout. But Gunn had avoide[d] that trail and had, instead, ridden around the canyo[n] rim. From this vantage point he could see the tra[il] leading up to the cabin, and he realized what mad[e] the cabin valuable as a hideout. Anyone approachin[g] the cabin would have two hundred yards of ope[n] territory to cross before they could actually get to th[e] house.

"All right, Esquire, here's where we separate th[e] goats from the men. Only right now, I'd kind'a like t[o] be a goat," Gunn said softly. He took a deep breath[,] rubbed his hands together, then started over the side[.]

Caitlin was tied to a chair. Taylor and Hargis wer[e] at the windows, looking out at the trail which ap[-]proached the cabin. Taylor and Hargis each had [a] Winchester in their hands, and another fully-loade[d] Winchester leaning against the wall beside them.

"You see anything?" Taylor asked, peering anx[-]iously through the window on his side.

"I don't see a damn thing," Hargis answered.

"I don't like it," Taylor said.

"Hell, maybe he ain't gonna come."

"He'll come," Taylor said. "He won't want anythin[g] to happen to this little ole' gal, here. Especially sinc[e] he done took a bath with her." Taylor chuckled, an[d] rubbed himself, then turned away from the window t[o] look at Caitlin. "You didn't know we seen you, di[d] you?"

Caitlin's face flamed red in embarrassment. "Yo[u]

ad no right to spy on me," she said.

"Of course we had the right. Your papa told us to eep our eye on you. He said you'd lead us to Gunn, nd you did. Then, when you went into the bathroom ith him, me 'n Hargis went in the room next door. hey's a hole there the bellboys use for watchin' the omen bathe, and we peeked through it."

"Yeah," Hargis said. "Only we seen a lot more'n a oman bathin'. You and him was really goin' at it."

"You're disgusting," Caitlin said. "Both of you are isgusting."

"Maybe so, but we didn't hump nobody in a public athroom," Taylor said.

"Taylor! I think I see somethin'!" Hargis spoke narply, and they both peered intently through the indow again.

"What is it?" Taylor asked.

After a moment, Hargis sighed. "It weren't othin'," he said. "Only a tree branch movin', that's ll. Why don't he come?"

"He's not going to come," Caitlin said. "You've asted your time."

"You better hope he comes," Taylor replied. "Else ou're gonna be the one to suffer from it."

It was very hard going. Gunn had been at it for half n hour, and the cabin was still as small as it had been hen he started down the canyon wall. He was now inging to the side, moving only when he could find ie tiniest handhold, the smallest crevice for a foot. n three sides of him was nothing but air, and if he issed a hand or a foothold, he had a drop of a quarter of a mile to the rocks below.

Sweat was pouring into Gunn's eyes. It was funn[y] just half an hour ago he had been blowing on h[is] hands to keep them warm.

The sweat wasn't all brought on by exertion . . some of it was brought about by worry. Now, fo[r] example. He had just about reached an impasse. H[e] had reached a bulge in the canyon wall, and ha[d] negotiated four-fifths of the way around it, but fo[r] the last five minutes he had been unable to go on[,] because he couldn't find another foothold.

Reluctantly, Gunn decided to climb back up. H[e] would have to approach the cabin by the trail afte[r] all. It would mean he would risk being seen, but hi[s] alternative was to fall to a certain death.

Gunn reached for the handhold he had surrendere[d] five minutes earlier, the first step in retracing hi[s] path. He had a good handhold, then he started t[o] move his foot to climb. But this time the small slat[e] outcropping which had supported his weight earlie[r] failed, and with a sickening sensation in his stomach[,] he felt himself falling. He threw himself against th[e] side, scraping and tearing at his flesh. He flaile[d] against the wall with his hands, and after a drop o[f] some fifteen feet, found a sturdy cottonwood tre[e.] The tree supported his weight and he hung there for [a] moment, looking down between his feet at the cabi[n] roof, far below. He saw the slate outcropping whic[h] had broken under his weight, still in free fall. [A] couple of seconds later he saw the little puff of dus[t] as it struck the roof of the cabin.

"What the hell was that?" Hargis asked, startled by the sound.

"Don't worry about it. It was probably an icicle or something like that. Stuff is fallin' on this roof all the time," Taylor said.

"I don't like it," Hargis said. "I think we ought to check it out."

"All right, be my guest," Taylor said. "You step out there and look up on the roof. Then if Gunn is hidin' in the rocks out there and sees you, maybe I can see the smoke from his rifle when he shoots."

"What? What are you talking about?"

"You want to make yourself a target for Gunn?"

"No."

"Then don't worry about an icicle or a dirt-clod fallin' on the roof. I told you, it happens all the time."

"Yeah," Hargis said. He laughed nervously. "Yeah, I guess it does. I remember when I first started comin' up here, I sometimes got to thinkin' someone was walkin' around on the roof."

"You just gotta remember that there ain't no way anyone can even get to the roof without comin' up that trail first. And either me or you have had our eyes on it from the time we got here."

Hargis levered a new bullet into his rifle. It was purely a nervous reaction, because there was already a round in the chamber, and his action kicked the first bullet out. It landed with a solid clunk on the cabin floor.

"Will you calm down," Taylor directed.

Gunn looked to his right. About four feet away

from him there was a narrow shelf. If he could gain that shelf he would be all right. He took a deep breath, then swung his feet toward it, catching the ledge with the heel of his boot. Slowly, he worked himself up, pushing away from the cottonwood tree until his knees were also on the ledge. Finally he let go of the tree altogether, and worked himself up until, at last, he was on the ledge. With the ledge to start from, he began his descent once more. As he got farther down on the wall, he began to find more hand and footholds, until, finally, the climb became almost as easy as climbing down a ladder. Less than ten minutes later, he was able to step off onto the roof of the cabin.

Gunn moved as quietly as he could. When he reached the edge, he lay down, then sticking his head over, found that he could see through a gap in the logs between the top of the wall and the eave of the roof. His vision was somewhat restricted, and there wasn't enough space to shoot through the gap, but he could see well enough to find out what was going on.

The first thing he saw was that Caitlin was tied up. In an odd way, he felt good about that. He knew such treatment had to be uncomfortable for her, and he was sorry about that, but he was glad that she wasn't a party to whatever these men were doing. O'Toole's daughter or not, she seemed to be an innocent victim of circumstances.

Taylor and Hargis were at the two windows in front of the cabin. There were only three entrances to the whole cabin . . . the front door and the two front windows. And with Taylor and Hargis standing vigil, there was no way for him to get in, even if he had been able to get this far without being seen.

Gunn raised himself back up and began looking around the cabin, trying to find some way of getting in, or at least getting into a position to shoot at them. As he stood there, a change in the wind brought the smoke from the stovepipe whipping toward him, and, trapped in the smoke was a little piece of burning ember. Gunn slapped at it as it landed on him. Then suddenly, he had an idea.

Gunn crossed the roof again, as softly and quietly as he could. He reached the chimney, which was really no more than a stretch of pipe which reached up from the stove below. A small, umbrella-like hood was over the top of the smokestack to prevent rain from putting out the fire, but there was about a two inch separation from the bottom edge of the umbrella and the top of the smokestack . . . plenty of room for him to do what needed to be done.

Gunn fingered six bullets from their loops in his belt, and held them in his hand. He looked at them for a moment, then dropped them down the smoke-stack, into the stove below. After that he moved quickly to the front edge of the roof, lay down and waited.

Caitlin heard something fall into the stove, but she had no idea what it could be. It didn't sound like the normal popping of woodgas. Whatever it was, she wasn't going to mention it to Taylor and Hargis, who were still glued to the front windows.

Suddenly a series of explosions came from the stove. They were loud, and terrifying, and one of them caused the stovepipe to burst open.

"What the hell!" Taylor shouted, and he and Hargis both turned away from the windows.

At the moment Gunn heard the first explosion, he was ready for action. Putting his hands on the edge of the roof he did a roll, right over the edge of the roof, then crashed, feet first on the porch. He drew his pistol, dove headlong through the window and into the room. The explosion of the bullets in the stove, and his equally explosive entry to the room, so disoriented Taylor and Hargis that by the time they swung their rifles, Gunn was already cocking his pistol.

Both Taylor and Hargis got off a shot, but both their shots were wild. Gunn fired two times. His first bullet smashed into Taylor's heart, his second made a hole where Hargis' nose had been. There were three final, but simultaneous explosions from the rounds Gunn had dropped into the stove.

"Are you all right?" Gunn asked, barely able to see Caitlin through the billowing smoke from the fight.

"Yes," Caitlin answered. "Yes, I'm fine."

Gunn slipped his pistol back into his holster, then started loosening the ropes which held Caitlin bound to the chair.

"Nice friends your father has," Gunn said.

"They're just doing what he asked them to do," Caitlin said.

Gunn looked at her. He had known that, but he didn't want to tell her. No matter how evil a man Jake O'Toole might be, he was still her father.

"You don't have to protect me," Caitlin said. "I know about him. I know all about him now. Taylor and Hargis spared me none of the details. I know that he has been raiding innocent Indian camps, murdering miners for their diggings, and . . . oh, Gunn, is it true? Did my father really attack a wagon and kill an entire family?"

Gunn sighed and shook his head. "I'm afraid it is true," he said.

"And to think that I was nearly ready to believe him when he told me all those lies about my mother," Caitlin said. She began to cry then, and Gunn put his arms around her to hold her and comfort her.

Caitlin cried bitter tears for several moments, as she stood there, cradled in Gunn's powerful, comforting arms. Finally she forced all the remorse and bitterness out of her system, and she pulled herself together. The crying stopped and she wiped her eyes.

"I'm sorry," she apologized. "You won't see me cry again. No matter what happens, I'll not cry again."

"You had every right to cry, Caitlin," Gunn said. "If ever anyone has been handed a sour apple in life, it's you."

"Gunn?"

"Yes?"

"You're going to kill my father, aren't you?"

Gunn turned away from Caitlin and looked at the bodies of the two men on the floor.

"I'll give him a chance to surrender to the law," Gunn said.

"And if he doesn't? If he tries to make a fight of it, you'll have to kill him."

"I'm afraid so," he said.

"I . . . I would like to try and talk him into surrendering," Caitlin said. "Would you mind if I try?"

"I don't mind if you try," Gunn said. "But I don't give it much chance."

"But I can try," Caitlin said.

"You try, then I'll try. But before I let him get away, I'll kill him."

"I understand. Do what you have to do," she said. "You'll get no trouble from me."

"Come on," Gunn invited. "Let's get back into town."

"Where's your horse? How did you get here?"

"My horse is up on the rim," Gunn said. "We'll pick him up on the way out. We'll ride out on their horses." He glanced at the dead men a last time.

A few minutes later, Gunn and Caitlin started up the trail that led out of the canyon. When they reached the first stand of trees, Gunn twisted around in his saddle and looked back at the cabin. Had he tried a frontal assault, he would have had this much open territory to cross before he reached them. The cabin walls were thick logs which could turn away anything short of a twelve pound cannon ball, and whoever was inside would have been perfectly safe. Gunn would have never made it, had he not come down the canyon wall.

"Gunn? Gunn, there's someone coming down the trail!" Caitlin hissed quickly, and Gunn turned back around with his pistol in his hand. When he saw the figure coming down the trail, he chuckled.

"Well, I'll be damned," he said.

"Who is it?"

"Smoke Eyes," Gunn said.

"Who?"

"Smoke Eyes. She's an Indian friend of mine. And she's leading Esquire."

"Shadow Hand," Smoke Eyes greeted as they came closer together. Gunn smiled as he noticed she was now using the name the Sioux had given him.

"Hello, Smoke Eyes."

"I have brought you your horse."

"Thanks. Oh, Smoke Eyes, I'd like you to meet a friend. This is Caitlin. Caitlin, Smoke Eyes."

Smoke Eyes looked at Caitlin with an expression that was totally blank. If there was jealousy, she did a good job of masking it. Caitlin's expression was more curious than anything else.

"What are you doing here, Smoke Eyes?" Gunn asked.

"The men here are the men who murdered my people, yes?"

"Yes," Gunn said.

"I came to watch them die."

"You're a little late."

"I was not too late. I watched you climb down the mountain. I heard the shooting. I knew Shadow Hand would win."

Gunn smiled. "I appreciate your confidence," he said.

"Now, there is only one more."

"My father?" Caitlin asked.

The composed expression on Smoke Eyes' face evaporated and she looked at Caitlin in surprise.

"Her father?"

"Jacob O'Toole," Gunn said.

Smoke Eyes' brow furrowed, and she narrowed her eyes.

"Why have you become friends with our enemy?" she asked.

"Caitlin is not our enemy," Gunn said. "She is not her father."

"She is her father's blood," Smoke Eyes insisted. "If you kill her father, she will have to kill you."

"No," Gunn explained. "The white man doesn't feel that way. We feel that each person has a choice. Caitlin is not responsible for anything her father does."

"She will try to prevent us from taking revenge against her father," Smoke Eyes said.

"No," Caitlin insisted. "I won't, really I won't. I would like to see him brought to trial."

"No," Smoke Eyes said. "No trial. O'Toole must die."

Chapter Fifteen

Gunn, Caitlin and Smoke Eyes rode past the house of Nancy Venable as they came into Deadwood. Gunn remembered the night he had spent with Nancy . . . remembered their love-making, and her innocence. He glanced toward the house, and saw that a towel was still hanging on the clothesline out back. The sight of that towel, unmoved since it was hung up by a now-dead girl, reinforced Gunn's determination to settle accounts with Jacob O'Toole. He had promised Caitlin that he would attempt to bring O'Toole to justice, if O'Toole didn't resist. He hoped O'Toole would resist.

By the time the three riders reached the outer limits of Deadwood, word that they were coming had already spread through the town. Men and women were coming out of houses, stores, hotels, restaurants and saloons to watch the arrival. They stood on the boardwalks and out in the streets, sometimes grouped as many as four or five deep, watching silently as the little trio rode by.

Despite the fact that there were now hundreds of

people out on the streets, the only sound to be heard was the hollow, echoing clip-clop of the horses' hooves. The sight of so many people just standing there in absolute silence was eerie, and the horses became nervous. They fidgeted and skidded, and once Smoke Eyes horse whinnied and turned completely around on her. She made soothing, clucking sounds to her animal, and finally got him under control.

"Gunn?" Caitlin said. She looked at the silent people. "What is it? Why are all these people here? Why are they so . . . so silent?"

"I imagine the story got around that I was going after you," Gunn answered. "The fact that we came back tells what happened to the two men who had you. There's only one man left now, and they know it."

"It's . . . it's frightening," Caitlin said.

"Gunn! Gunn!" someone called, and Gunn stopped and looked toward Weiner.

"What is it, Weiner?" Gunn asked.

"O'Toole," Weiner said. "He's in the Deadwood Saloon, waitin' for you."

"Is he planning to drygulch me?"

"He says he wants to have it out with you, fair and square," Weiner said. "But, well, I'd be careful if I was you."

"Obliged for the warning," Gunn said, touching his hat. He and the two women with him resumed their ride down the long main street, toward the Deadwood Saloon. Gunn caught a blur of movement out of the corner of his eye and when he looked over, he saw half a dozen little boys, running excitedly along the length of the boardwalk, keeping up with Gunn so they would be in on the action.

Gunn reached the hitching rail in front of the saloon, then swung down from Esquire and tied his horse off. He looked toward the saloon doors and saw Alves' bald head above the batwings. Gunn started for the door, and the crowd of people standing between Gunn and the front of the saloon opened up, like the sea parting for Moses. Gunn pushed inside. Smoke Eyes and Caitlin came with him.

There, at the far end of the bar, stood Jake O'Toole, calmly drinking a glass of whiskey.

"Well, now, 'n if it isn't the fine Mr. Gunn, 'n with two lovely lassies in tow," O'Toole said.

There were at least three dozen people in the saloon, but all conversation halted, the drinking stopped, and every eye was wide to the drama which was about to play itself out between these two men.

"Alves, it's been a cold, dry ride," Gunn said. "I want some whiskey. And if you try and serve me any of that rotgut you served me the last time, I'm going to be very angry."

"I . . . I've got some good stuff," Alves said nervously.

"Aye, nothin' but the best for my friend, Gunn," O'Toole said. "I hear I've you to thank for the rescue of my own darlin' daughter."

"You're thanking him for rescuing me, when it was you who had me captured?" Caitlin spat.

O'Toole smiled, and held his hands up, palm out. "Oh, my darlin', to think you'd be believin' such a thing about your own father. Why, I was that worried about you I was talkin' to Alves here about puttin' up a reward for your safe return. Am I right, Alves?"

"Y . . . Yes, sir, that's right," Alves said. Alves' hand was shaking so badly that he could barely pour the whiskey.

"Shut up, Alves," Gunn said quietly.

"Y . . . Yes, sir. I'll shut up," Alves said. He tried to hand the glass to Gunn, but he was shaking so badly he couldn't hold it. He put it on the bar and slid it across. Gunn picked it up, and O'Toole poured himself another glass.

"You had your daughter taken, O'Toole. And you murdered Nancy Venable and her father, and the people on that wagon, and who knows how many others."

"Those are strong accusations you're makin', Gunn. You don't really think you can prove all that, do you?"

Gunn chuckled dryly. "Prove it? What do you think I am, a court of law? I don't have to prove it, you son of a bitch, all I have to do is believe it."

The confident smile left O'Toole's face for a second, then, as if composing himself with effort, he smiled again. O'Toole held his glass out in a toast. "To you, Mr. Gunn," he said. He tossed the drink down. "I suppose you're about to shoot me down, now?"

"I would like to. But I promised your daughter I'd give you a chance to surrender yourself to the law."

"Well, bless me now, so my own darlin' daughter actually worried about that, did she?" O'Toole said. He put his hand on his heart. "Sure'n I'm touched, lass, truly touched. But tell me true, would you be wantin' to see your own papa climb those terrible

200

thirteen steps to the hangman's gallows? Why, girl, I'd be kissin' the devil's ass before the rope stopped swingin'."

"You could get a fair trial," Caitlin suggested.

O'Toole laughed. "Fair, you say? Darlin', that's just the point, don't you see? If it's fair, I'm sure to hang. No, I'd rather go down fightin'."

With those words, there was a scrape of tables and chairs as the saloon patrons suddenly decided there was a safer place to be than the middle of a battleground. They wanted a safer place, but they didn't want to give up their vantage points, so they hurried to the walls and the far side of the stove, to be out of the line of fire, but still able to watch. Alves left his position behind the bar and hurried over to join the others.

"You women get out of the way," Gunn said, waving them to one side.

"Gunn, before we start," O'Toole said. "I would like you to be noticin' that I'm not wearin' a gun."

"I'm not interested in a fist fight," Gunn said.

"Nor am I, lad, nor am I," O'Toole replied. He reached around behind his belt and pulled out a knife. "I'd like to carve you up a bit."

"I don't have a knife." The Mexican knife was in his saddlebag, he realized.

O'Toole smiled, then snapped the knife forward with a rapid flick of his wrist. It stuck into the floor about two inches in front of Gunn's boot, quivering rapidly, making a little swishing sound as the handle moved back and forth. "Now you do," O'Toole said. The Irishman pulled another knife, a twin to the one he threw at Gunn, from his coat.

Gunn unfastened his gunbelt and handed it to Caitlin, then he leaned over and pulled the knife from the floor of the saloon. It came out with a snap, and he assumed a stance similar to O'Toole's. Gunn was crouched a little, right arm out, blade projecting from across the upturned palm between the thumb and index finger, with the point moving back and forth, slowly and hypnotically.

O'Toole danced in, lightly for a heavy man, and raised his left hand toward Gunn's face to mask his action. He feinted with his right, the knife hand, outside Gunn's left arm as if he were going to go in over it. In the same movement, when Gunn automatically raised his left arm to block, O'Toole brought his knife hand back down so fast it was a blur, and he went in under Gunn's arm.

The knife seared Gunn's flesh like a branding iron along his ribs, and opened a long gash in the tight ridges of muscle. The cut began to spill bright red blood through the slice in his shirt, and over the belt of his trousers. Gunn brought his left hand down sharply, almost by reflex, and he knocked away the knife which O'Toole was now holding with an air of careless confidence. He jabbed quickly with his right hand, sending the blade of his knife into O'Toole's diaphragm, just under the ribs.

"Well, bless me now," O'Toole gasped, and he stepped back several paces away from Gunn and looked down in surprise at the wound in his belly. Suddenly he raised his arm again, and when he did, he was holding a derringer.

"Shadow Hand!" Smoke Eyes shouted, seeing the little hold-out pistol before anyone else. She rushed toward O'Toole just as O'Toole fired. She went down with her chest pumping blood.

"No!" Gunn shouted, and he closed the distance between them, grabbing the derringer as O'Toole tried to discharge the second shot. They wrestled in heavy-breathed silence for a moment, then Gunn began to get the edge. He pulled the gun away from O'Toole's hands and rammed the barrel into O'Toole's mouth, pushing it so far down his throat that he began to gag. Gunn pulled the trigger, and the heavy .41 caliber ball smashed through the back of O'Toole's head, splattering the front and top of the bar with blood, brain-matter and chips of bone. O'Toole slid down, supported in the sitting position by the bar. His head was back, his eyes open, and the handle of the pistol was protruding from his mouth like the butt of a well-chewed cigar.

Caitlin screamed, and twisted away from the scene in horror. Gunn dropped on one knee beside Smoke Eyes. She looked up at him and smiled, weakly.

"I can tell my sister, my brother, my people who have gone before me, that justice is done," she said.

Gunn looked up. "Get a doctor," he said. "Somebody get a doctor."

"I'm a doctor," someone said.

The doctor was an old man, with white hair and a white beard and moustache. He knelt down to look at Smoke Eyes, felt her pulse, then shook his head slowly.

"There's nothing I can do for her," he said. "She's dead." The doctor reached toward Gunn's side, but Gunn pushed his hand away.

"No," he said. "I'll take care of it myself."

"Yes, I guess you can at that," the doctor said. "It's not very deep. But I know you can feel the pain."

"Doc," Gunn said, standing up then and buckling his gunbelt back on. He winced as the belt passed across his wound. "You have no idea of the pain I feel."

Gunn walked out of the saloon, climbed onto Esquire.

Caitlin looked at him a moment, then climbed atop her own pony. She rode to the end of the street, then spurred her mount into a full gallop. Gunn turned Esquire's head in the opposite direction, put the horse into a canter. He rode past the gawkers and the curious children.

The hatred that had boiled up in him began to simmer and cool as he cleared the town, a sadder, wiser man than he had been when he arrived.

WHITE SQUAW
Zebra's Adult Western Series
by E.J. Hunter

#1: SIOUX WILDFIRE   (1205, $2.50)

#2: BOOMTOWN BUST   (1286, $2.50)

#3: VIRGIN TERRITORY   (1314, $2.50)

#4: HOT TEXAS TAIL   (1359, $2.50)

#5: BUCKSKIN BOMBSHELL   (1410, $2.50)

#6: DAKOTA SQUEEZE   (1479, $2.50)

#7: ABILENE TIGHT SPOT   (1562, $2.50)

#8: HORN OF PLENTY   (1649, $2.50)

#9: TWIN PEAKS — OR BUST   (1746, $2.50)

#10: SOLID AS A ROCK   (1831, $2.50)

Available wherever paperbacks are sold, or order direct from the Publisher. Send cover price plus 50¢ per copy for mailing and handling to Zebra Books, Dept. 1914, 475 Park Avenue South, New York, N.Y. 10016. Residents of New York, New Jersey and Pennsylvania must include sales tax. DO NOT SEND CASH.

TALES OF THE OLD WEST

SPIRIT WARRIOR (1795, $2.50)
by G. Clifton Wisler
The only settler to survive the savage indian attack was a little boy. Although raised as a red man, every man was his enemy when the two worlds clashed—but he vowed no man would be his equal.

IRON HEART (1736, $2.25)
by Walt Denver
Orphaned by an indian raid, Ben vowed he'd never rest until he'd brought death to the Arapahoes. And it wasn't long before they came to fear the rider of vengeance they called . . . Iron Heart.

WEST OF THE CIMARRON (1681, $2.50)
by G. Clifton Wisler
Eric didn't have a chance revenging his father's death against the Dunstan gang until a stranger with a fast draw and a dark past arrived from West of the Cimarron.

HIGH LINE RIDER (1615, $2.50)
by William A. Lucky
In Guffey Creek, you either lived by the rules made by Judge Breen and his hired guns—or you didn't live at all. So when Holly took sides against the Judge, it looked like there would be just one more body for the buzzards. But this time they were wrong.

GUNSIGHT LODE (1497, $2.25)
by Virgil Hart
When Ned Coffee cornered Glass and Corey in a mine shaft, the last thing Glass expected was for the kid to make a play for the gold. And in a blazing three-way shootout, both Corey and Coffee would discover how lightening quick Glass was with a gun.

Available wherever paperbacks are sold, or order direct from the Publisher. Send cover price plus 50¢ per copy for mailing and handling to Zebra Books, Dept. 1914, 475 Park Avenue South, New York, N.Y. 10016. Residents of New York, New Jersey and Pennsylvania must include sales tax. DO NOT SEND CASH.

THE OMNI COLLECTION
from Zebra Books

THE OMNI BOOK OF SPACE (1275, $3.95)
Edited by Owen Davies
The OMNI BOOK OF SPACE offers 35 articles by some of the best known writers of our time, including Robert Heinlein, James Michener, and Ray Bradbury, which offer a guide to the research and engineering that can make our world a better place to live.

THE OMNI BOOK OF COMPUTERS
AND ROBOTS (1276, $3.95)
Edited by Owen Davies
They have become a part of our lives: at work and at home computers are being used more and more, and every day we see more evidence of the computer revolution. This fascinating book is available to answer all the questions and unravel the mystery.

THE OMNI BOOK OF MEDICINE (1364, $3.95)
Edited by Owen Davies
A life span of two hundred years? A world without pain? These medical advances—and many more—are right around the corner and are part of this remarkable collection of articles that will give you a glimpse of a healthier tomorrow.

THE OMNI BOOK OF PSYCHOLOGY (1868, $3.95)
Edited by Peter Tyson
Dreams, mind control, psychographics—these are the topics that can both excite and frighten all of us when we think about the techniques of psychology in the future. In this volume you will see how the barriers of human fear and high-tech anxiety will be broken.

THE OMNI BOOK OF HIGH-TECH
SOCIETY 2000 (1896, $3.95)
Edited by Peter Tyson
In a world of computer revolutions, new biomedical frontiers and alternative energy sources, where will you stand? You can match wits with Arthur C. Clarke by taking the quiz included in this book. Welcome to the future!

Available wherever paperbacks are sold, or order direct from the Publisher. Send cover price plus 50¢ per copy for mailing and handling to Zebra Books, Dept. 1914, 475 Park Avenue South, New York, N.Y. 10016. Residents of New York, New Jersey and Pennsylvania must include sales tax. DO NOT SEND CASH.

ASHES
by William W. Johnstone

OUT OF THE ASHES   (1137, $3.50)
Ben Raines hadn't looked forward to the War, but he knew it was coming. After the balloons went up, Ben was one of the survivors, fighting his way across the country, searching for his family, and leading a band of new pioneers attempting to bring American OUT OF THE ASHES.

FIRE IN THE ASHES   (1310, $3.50)
It's 1999 and the world as we know it no longer exists. Ben Raines, leader of the Resistance, must regroup his rebels and prep them for bloody guerrilla war. But are they ready to face an even fiercer foe—the human mutants threatening to overpower the world!

ANARCHY IN THE ASHES   (1387, $3.50)
Out of the smoldering nuclear wreckage of World War III, Ben Raines has emerged as the strong leader the Resistance needs. When Sam Hartline, the mercenary, joins forces with an invading army of Russians, Ben and his people raise a bloody banner of defiance to defend earth's last bastion of freedom.

BLOOD IN THE ASHES   (1537, $3.50)
As Raines and his rugged band of followers search for land that has escaped radiation, the insidious group known as The Ninth Order rises up to destroy them. In a savage battle to the death, it is the fate of America itself that hangs in the balance!

ALONE IN THE ASHES   (1721, $3.50)
In this hellish new world there are human animals and Ben Raines—famed soldier and survival expert—soon becomes their hunted prey. He desperately tries to stay one step ahead of death, but no one can survive ALONE IN THE ASHES.

Available wherever paperbacks are sold, or order direct from the Publisher. Send cover price plus 50¢ per copy for mailing and handling to Zebra Books, Dept. 1914, 475 Park Avenue South, New York, N.Y. 10016. Residents of New York, New Jersey and Pennsylvania must include sales tax. DO NOT SEND CASH.